THE
POLFERRY
RIDDLE

THE POLFERRY RIDDLE

BY PHILIP MacDONALD

VINTAGE BOOKS
A DIVISION OF RANDOM HOUSE
NEW YORK

First Vintage Books Edition, September 1983
Copyright 1931 by Doubleday, Doran &
Company Inc. All rights reserved under
International and Pan-American Copyright
Conventions. Published in the United States by
Random House, Inc., New York, and
simultaneously in Canada by Random House
of Canada Limited, Toronto. Originally
published by Doubleday, Doran & Company,
Inc. in 1931.

Library of Congress Cataloging in Publication Data
MacDonald, Philip.
The Polferry riddle.
Reprint. Originally published:
Garden City, N.Y. : Doubleday, Doran, c1931.
I. Title.
PR6025.A2218P6 1983   823'.912   83-5807
ISBN 0-394-71711-2

Manufactured in the United States of America

THE
POLFERRY
RIDDLE

CHAPTER ONE

"SHUT it, man! Shut it!" said Trenchard. His heavy, swarthy face screwed itself up almost ludicrously. He pulled a handkerchief from his breast pocket and mopped at his neck and his left cheek. The storm-driven rain, as Banner had opened the window, had come clean across the long room; drops had spattered into the fire, other drops were the cause of the handkerchief.

Banner shut the window. He had some difficulty, but managed it at last.

"Dirty night!" he said.

Hale-Storford laughed; a joyous sound. He was at a side table, fiddling with decanter and glasses. He said:

"It's a good night. If one's inside. . . . Have another, Banner? And you, Trenchard?"

Banner brought his bulk back to the fire, walking with the heavy-seeming but light-sounding waddle of the old sailor. He let himself down into his chair with a grunt. The sound was at once affirmative answer to his host's question and an expression of pleasure—almost delight—at once more being seated.

"Thanks," said Trenchard

Hale-Storford gave them their glasses; came to them with a siphon. "Say when."

They said it. Banner, with an impatient-seeming twist of his neat iron-gray beard, almost before the siphon had begun to hiss; Trenchard when the whisky was noticeably paler.

Hale-Storford mixed his own. He said, glass in right hand, broad shoulders leaning against the corner of the oak mantel:

"Yes, a damn *good* night if one's inside. . . . D'you know, Banner, that's why I took this place?"

Banner grunted.

Hale-Storford laughed. "Dare say it wouldn't appeal to you. Though I'm not so sure of that. But it does appeal to me. It's nights like this—in this sort of place—that make a house a thing to take joy in and not just a place to use. What do you say?" He looked at Trenchard with the last words. Trenchard shrugged; a half smile lit up faintly his heavy face, which most of the time seemed to express, unwillingly, its owner's anger with the world and the ways of the world. Banner grunted again; his oversolid body seemed to be straining his clothes of gray flannel almost beyond endurance. He said:

"Always the way with you fellows that've lived in a town. Good God! I've seen enough dirty weather in my time to last me forever. What *I* really ought to have is a nice little house called 'Mon Repos,' with trams running by the door every other minute. Some place like Palmer's Green." He grunted again. "Instead . . ."

Hale-Storford put his fair head back and laughed again. "Instead you potter about inside and outside the estuary all day, every day, in a little one-ton ketch that ought to've drowned you long ago. You can't fool me!"

Trenchard laughed now. "Got him there! Though I must say he didn't want to go out this evening. I made him."

"Made hell!" Banner grunted. "Only reason

I went out is because I couldn't trust a hog-walloping lubber like you not to drown your-self. And see where your damned trip landed us! If Hale-Storford hadn't just taken this house, where'd we've been? I'll tell you—wet through and through and then through from the back again, and trudging four miles up the estu-ary to get to the coastguard's place. And I'll tell you what would've happened then, Ralph, my boy! Instead of having a nice sissy silk shirt and a pair of striped flannel bags and a nice chair and more whisky-and-sodas than're good for you—an' a lot of charmin' women to talk to until half an hour ago—you'd have been sitting in front of a fire that belched out smoke at you at every other breath, drinking brown tea out of a cup as thick as that bookcase, and wearing a pair of reach-me-down trousers over your lower parts and a scrubby guernsey next your chest!"

Trenchard grinned. "But our host *had* taken the house; *was* here; *did* happen to see our bit of bad luck."

Banner tossed his bulk about in his chair. "Bit

of bad luck! Bit of blasted landlubberly sailing!" His grunts were a crescendo. "The only place you ought to handle a boat, Ralph, is on the Serpentine on Sunday afternoons. *With* braces."

"You finish that whisky," said Hale-Storford, "and shut up grumbling. As Trenchard said, I was here; I had just taken the house, and there you are. And I expect you'd have done just the same thing with that boat yourself. Looks a sow of a thing, anyhow!" He paused for a moment; surveyed his unexpected guests.

Trenchard cut in. "All the same," he said, "luck or no luck, it's damn decent of you to put up with us like this."

"Decent nothing," said Hale-Storford. "I'm no good at pretence. Too busy generally, I suppose; got out of the habit. Damn pleased to see you. . . . I say, you know, most extraordinary coincidence, you knowing Eve."

Trenchard nodded. He did not speak.

"Damn funny, really," Hale-Storford went on. For a moment his usual eager, curt incisiveness had changed to a slower, wondering tone.

"To pick up a couple of fellows on one's own beach and find that you'd known one of 'em for twenty years'd be odd enough, but when you find the other's known your wife for—well, I suppose it must be nearly as long, acording to what you were saying—then it's *damn* funny!"

Trenchard spoke now. "Oh, it's not twenty years! Steady on a bit! I first knew Eve when she was ten, and that can't be more than fourteen years ago. . . . But it *is* queer. . . . I don't mind what happens, though. So long as nobody says, 'It shows what a small place this world is.'"

"Nobody's likely to here," said Hale-Storford, "except Uncle Percy there. I'll brain him if he does."

"Give me another shot of that whisky," Banner said, "and you can do what you like. How long've you been married? Never read the papers."

Hale-Storford took the empty glass held out to him; crossed to the tray-laden table. He said, pouring whisky:

"Six months. If I'd had my way it'd have been eighteen. But six months it is."

"And after six months you come down to a benighted, God-forsaken, devil-blistered part of the world like this!"

Hale-Storford brought back the glass, filled again. "Take this," he said. "And anyhow, you live here, don't you?"

Banner grunted assent. "But I hog it in a cottage, and nobody takes any notice of me, and I don't take any notice of them. But what do you think you swagger people are going to do . . ." He paused; held up a hand for silence. "Listen to that!" A wild scurry of rain which sounded against the leaded windows like handfuls of grapeshot thrown by angry gods broke the small silence into a thousand pieces. And then, as the rain squall died down, there came again the monotonous howling screech of the wind, below and beneath it the steady, unsubdued "hish-hish" of the sea.

Once more Hale-Storford laughed—a big, alert, trim man. Happiness and well-being irradiated him. "But I've told you I like it. Eve likes it. That's why we took the house. If we hadn't liked it we shouldn't be here. Eve found it; Eve wanted it; and as soon as I saw it I wanted it too. . . ."

"Accommodating husband!" said Banner.

"Accommodating nothing! Eve and I don't always agree, thank God! . . . Fancy living with someone who always agreed with you! . . . but we do over this. . . . She's going to be happy here and so am I."

Trenchard interrupted. "There's one thing, though, you won't get any servants."

Hale-Storford raised his eyebrows. "Think so? We've got two, anyhow. Man and wife. They're coming on Monday. And then there's Mrs. Greye—you met her—she's our sort of housekeeper, you know. That ought to be enough for this place; Eve's arranged for what I think they call 'daily help' from the village."

Banner set down his glass upon the floor beside him with a little thump. His neat beard twitched to a tremendous yawn. His bulk stirred lethargically. He said:

"Bed soon, if you don't mind."

"Have a nightcap?" said Hale-Storford.

"We-el . . ." The gray beard twitched again. "If you make me. . . ."

Once more the trip to the little table. At it Hale-Storford turned. "You, Trenchard?"

Trenchard shook his head. His dark face had relapsed once more into its usual expression of heavy gloom. He said abruptly:

"Who's that kid? Boy at dinner? He staying here?"

Hale-Storford squirted soda into the glass he was manipulating. "Yes. Young cousin of mine. Just left Ripton. Going to Caius just after Christmas. Nice kid." He came back with the glass; handed it to Banner; received in return for the glass a grunt almost ecstatic; went back to rest his shoulders once more against the mantel. He looked down at Trenchard asprawl in his chair. He said:

"I say! I'm very sorry, I probably made a muck of the introductions. Generally do. If you'd like to get straight before to-morrow . . . Well, there's Eve. You know her, of course.

Ha! You've known her longer than I have. Then the tall, dark, handsome woman's her sister. You must know her, by the way."

Trenchard shook his head. "So that's Eve's sister, is it?"

"Yes. And the little fair, silent person—she's not nearly so silent when you know her—that's Susan Kerr, friend of Eve's. And the tall, dignified one, that's Dorothy Graye, our housekeeper. She's had rotten luck. First husband killed in the war; second husband a rotter. He was drowned last year in the *Megantic,* and a good job too, I should say. But he had all her money. . . ."

"Interesting bag!" Trenchard's smile, lighting up the gloom of his face as he spoke, robbed the words of any incivility. Hale-Storford's quick smile came in answer; that quick smile which made his usually gravely perfect face into a pleasant, good-looking boy's. He said:

"Glad you think so."

Banner interrupted. Once more he put down an empty glass with a little thump. He said, looking at Trenchard:

"And he's left out the most interesting one. That's himself. Not often you're such a big bug in the bug world as Dick here. Not at his age, anyhow. What are you, son? Thirty-six?"

"Eight," said Hale-Storford. With one of those quick, somehow ultra-decisive movements he turned, took his own empty glass from the mantelpiece behind him, walked across the room, and set it down upon the tray. He said, from the table:

"Still feel like bed, uncle?"

"Uncle yourself! But you're right." Banner heaved his heaviness out of his chair. "Come on, Ralph!"

Trenchard rose. Hale-Storford opened the door. It led out onto the great high hall of the old house. A lamp burnt dimly on a table in the far corner. It sent flickering shadows over the black immensity. As the door opened a gust of wind shook the house from end to end. There were a thousand rattles, a thousand groans; wailings from the eaves and chimneys as the wind eddied round and down them. Banner said into the darkness:

"If this is the sort of night you like, you can keep it!"

"Sssh!" said Hale-Storford. And then, in a whisper: "Sorry! But those girls are tired out. We've only had Mrs. Graye and they've been doing all the work and humping furniture like a lot of men. . . . If you wouldn't mind coming up as quietly as you can . . . there's no carpet yet."

He led them silently into the half light. They saw him at the table with the lamp, and then the lamp's flickering paleness blaze up to a steady yellow light. He picked it up and came back toward them.

"Come along after me," he said.

They followed. At the foot of the stairs Trenchard stopped. They stood in a little group. Trenchard said:

"I say! Where're those dogs of yours?"

Hale-Storford raised his eyebrows. In the lamplight his face looked almost unreasonably boyish. He said:

"They're about. Don't you worry. I've introduced you."

Trenchard grinned and shrugged. "If you say so," he said. "But they're not little 'uns. I was just wondering if they'd resent a stranger answering a call in the middle of the night." He dropped his voice at the end of the sentence to a whisper. "Sorry!" he said. "Didn't mean to make a row."

"That's all right," said Hale-Storford. But his voice also was a whisper. He began to lead the way upstairs. He said over his shoulder:

"Eve was terribly tired to-night."

They went up the wide uncarpeted oak staircase. They trod like cats, but under their feet the creakings were like pistol shots. Banner grunted. Trenchard swore beneath his breath. Hale-Storford kept on. He said at the top:

"Damn place sounds like a barrage."

Banner whispered, looking about him in the shadows of the three-sided gallery which was the house's upper floor.

"That noise won't wake anyone. Not if they can sleep through the blow. Just listen to it! Will you listen!"

The wind seemed to have doubled its

strength. It tore at the house. It shook the house. It seemed to howl and shriek with fury at the failure of its efforts upon the house.

"God!" said Hale-Storford. Then: "Come on, you fellows!" He spoke in a low voice less carrying than any whisper. "First door's my sister-in-law's. . . . This one's Susan Kerr's. . . . This next one's Eve's and mine." He halted. "There're your two, next each other."

He held the lamp over his head; he looked at his two guests. The soft yellow light made a bright pool in which they all stood. They were just outside the door he had pointed as his own. He said:

"Don't know how you'll fix it. One's a big room, t'other's small. Luckily we got the beds up to-day." He looked at Banner. "You'd better have the big one, hadn't you, uncle?"

"Uncle yourself!" said Banner. And then, staring at Trenchard: "Lord, man! What's up?"

Hale-Storford swung round. . . . The pool of light widened in a flickering circle.

Trenchard was staring at the floor. Not at that

part of the floor immediately beneath his feet or his comrades', but at the boards which were just inside the circle of the lamp's light, outside the bedroom door of his host. In the yellow glow his face showed as a pallid blotch. As he stared, his right arm rose—slowly, seemingly without conscious volition—to point a rigid finger.

"What's that?" His voice was a harsh, strident whisper.

Banner drew in his breath with a sharp hiss. He said roughly:

"Water. Don't be a damn fool! Water, I said. Somebody spilt some water."

Suddenly they stood, he and Trenchard, in the darkness. . . . But the door and the sluggish, barely glistening streak which seemed to come out from beneath it were bathed in the soft flood of light.

Hale-Storford was at the door. Hale-Storford set his fingers to the door and flung it open. . . .

They heard his voice. "Eve darling! . . . Eve! . . ."

Then, more dreadful than any sound, dead silence. . . .

In foul sympathy the wind had dropped until there was no sound. In the darkness old Banner felt fingers clutch his arm, digging painfully into his biceps. He could see into the room a little; the door was wide. He could see, reflected from the white ceiling, the yellow flood of the lamp.

And then a sound. A sound indescribable. A sound half stifled shout, half sob. The yellow flood of light swayed back, rushed through the doorway; sent flying the darkness between the doorway and the waiting men. . . .

Hale-Storford stood in that doorway. He was steady and still. Too steady, too still. . . .

Banner, with an impatient twitch of his arm, threw away those gripping fingers; took three steps forward.

"What's up, boy?" he said. "What's up?"

Hale-Storford spoke. He said:

"Trenchard, go downstairs. Telephone in the hall. On the table. Ring Polferry Police Station." And then dreadfully his voice seemed to go. His lips were moving, but no sound came.

Banner was close to him now, touching him,

gripping his coat and shaking him, saying still:

"What's up, boy? What's *up?*"

Hale-Storford's voice came back. It was not the same voice. It was a dead, flat sound. It said:

"Eve. Look!"

He turned; took two steps back into the room. Banner followed. In three strides Trenchard was behind them.

Hale-Storford stood, steady as if he had been carven from oak, holding the lamp unnaturally high above his head. . . .

"Oh, my God!" said Banner.

From behind him there came the sound of a stifled gasp. A voice came from beneath the lamp, the voice that should have been Hale-Storford's. It said:

"Trenchard! Telephone!"

Trenchard went. . . .

"Oh, my God!" said Banner again.

CHAPTER TWO

SUPERINTENDENT (LATE CHIEF DETECTIVE IN-
SPECTOR) ARNOLD PIKE of the Criminal Investi-
gation Department sat with his feet upon his
desk—feet clad in black boots of an abnormal
polish—and gazed out at the four square yards
of Thames which was his view. He was trying
to think of those poisoned sweetmeats which
had been sent to Jacqueline Roget. His thoughts
—as he had known they would when he began
them—got him nowhere along this line. They
persisted most obstinately in staying upon another. He whistled lugubriously and flatly between his teeth, switched his gaze from the bit
of river to the glistening toes of his boots, from
the toes of his boots to the river again. Nothing
happened. . . .

The telephone upon his table rang shrill. He
took his feet from the desk and the telephone

into his hands in one movement. He listened. He said, "Very good, sir. Right away, sir!" and put back the receiver upon its hook.

He stood up. He straightened his tie. He made one last, and unsuccessful, effort to clear his mind of that line of thought along which it had persisted in running and left his room. He went along the bare stone-floored corridor to the head of the stairs. He went down one flight of stairs. He turned to his right and knocked upon the third door on his left. He was, within two minutes, then in the presence of Assistant Commissioner Egbert Lucas.

Lucas was standing, hands in his pockets, by his window; a window which looked out upon much more river than did Pike's. He turned. He said:

"Morning, Pike! Sit down."

Pike sat. Lucas, a tall figure of early middle-aged immaculateness, lounged from the window to sit opposite. Lucas said, tilting back his swivel chair:

"Well, I've read it."

Pike waited.

"I've read it," Lucas said again. "Damn it, I've read it three times!"

"Yes, sir?" Pike was politely inquiring. "Which one, sir?"

"Don't be a fathead, Pike. Have a cigarette."

"Thank you, sir. You speaking like that, I suppose I'm to take you as meaning the Polferry job."

"Suppose be damned! You know perfectly well, Pike, that I *meant* the Polferry job." Lucas twisted uneasily in his chair, took a cigarette, lit it, threw it away after two puffs; said at last and irritably:

"Well, say something!"

Pike shrugged. "Nothing to say, sir."

"I know that. I've just read your report, haven't I? But I want to hear you say it. All over again."

It was Pike's turn to shift uneasily in his chair. He began to speak but was cut short by the burring of the telephone. Lucas picked it up.

"What's that? . . . Yes, Lucas speaking. Who? . . . Of course I can. Send him up at once. And you needn't ask another time. You ought to know that by now."

He put down the receiver and looked at Pike. A slow smile lightened the gloom. Pike smiled too, dutifully.

"That," Lucas said, "was to say that Colonel Gethryn wanted to see me."

Pike's smile changed from one of duty to one of reality.

They waited.

The door opened and there entered to them, in clothes of a pleasing brown and an easy elegance putting Lucas's studied effects to shame, the long person of Anthony Ruthven Gethryn.

They made much of him. A little, he thought —and said—too much. He sat—his favourite place in this room—upon the broad, low window sill. He smoked and waited. He did not have long to wait.

Lucas said: "Pike's just come down. We were talking about that Polferry business. Heard about it?"

Anthony grinned. "Not so much as I'm going

to hear. . . . Know what *I've* come for, Lucas?"

Lucas shook his head. "Not unless it's just to pass the time of day with the police."

"I have come," said Anthony, "to say good-bye. Good-bye, anyhow, for six or seven months. We're going away. There seems to be an idea prevalent in the medical profession that Mrs. Anthony Gethryn and Master Alan Gethryn would do better for themselves if they stopped filling their lungs with a mixture of soot and carbon monoxide. Air, sir, and pure air! is the doctor's cry. I must say I'm rather with 'em."

Lucas made unsuccessful effort to hide dismay. But he was brave. "Where is it, this air?"

"Switzerland," said Anthony. He smiled suddenly at Pike. "Now shoot! What were you saying—Polferry? Polferry? Where is it? Country? Let me see, that's where . . . doctors . . . I've got you! That young cancer fellow. Inquest still on. Wife had her head cut off."

Lucas began endeavour to make hay while the sun shone. "Read it up at all?" he said.

"Nary word. Never read the papers."

Lucas got up and began to wander about the room. "Pike," he said, "has been down there. I will say *that* for the Wessex Police: they asked us to help at once. They didn't wait until they'd mucked everything up."

Anthony looked at him, then at Pike. He said, to the air between them:

"Which worries us most? Getting nowhere or having to tell the Wessex Police that we've got nowhere?"

"Both, sir." Pike was glum.

"Yes, damn it!" Lucas agreed. "And it's so crazy, the whole thing."

"Is it now?" Anthony stood up and pitched his cigarette into the fire. "Bear to let Pike tell me?"

Lucas went back to his chair and sat down. "Could I *bear!*" he said. "Carry on, Pike!"

Pike looked glumly at his shining boots. Pike collected his thoughts. Pike said:

"Don't know whether you know that end of Wessex, sir. Polferry. Practically Cornwall. . . . This house is called the Watch House. It's right on the mouth of the river Starr. There's very high cliffs just where the sea begins, and this house—well, it's right up on top of the westmost cliff. And when I say right on top, sir, I mean right on top. Why, there's a drop outside the drawing-room window of the Losh knows how many hundreds of feet. . . . Right outside the window it is, sir. Very handy for cigarette ends and such like. Well, Dr. Hale-Storford —you know about him, sir; he's the young doctor that's made such a stir in this cancer research —well, sir, he took the Watch House matter of a month ago. Seems they wanted a quiet place in the country for himself and his wife. He's only been married about six months. Married a young lady called Rossiter—Eve Rossiter. Very happy couple, according to all accounts. Well, sir, they had to keep their London house on, so they'd left their regular servants up in London and got a man and wife who were going to come in in about three days after they took over the house. Dr. and Mrs. Hale-Storford took down with them Miss Miriam Rossiter— that's Mrs. Hale-Storford's sister; a young gentleman called Anstruther—George Anstruther, a cousin of Dr. Hale-Storford's; and Miss Susan Kerr—she's a friend of Mrs. Hale-Storford's; was at school with her; and a Mrs. Graye—Dorothy Graye. She's a lady, sir, who's apparently been unfortunate in her choice of partners and lost all her money. She's been housekeeper for Dr. and Mrs. Hale-Storford ever since they were married. I think it was Mrs. Hale-Storford's mother who got her the job.

"Well, sir, they took over the house on the seventeenth of November. By the morning of the eighteenth they'd got a bit straight. And then, on the second night, Mrs. Hale-Storford gets found by her husband with a great gash in her throat that's bled her to death.

"All very nice, sir. All very straightforward, *up* to there. Where it begins to get what you might call complicated is here. That house, sir, the Watch House, that's absolutely cut off, as you might say, from civilization. And Dr. Hale-Storford's got two big dogs—Great Danes, they are—very fine house dogs. They're in the hall and won't let even a black beetle come into the

house without letting everybody know it. The
house is locked. All windows, except in one
room which was occupied, are latched. All the
doors are bolted. The dogs are inside."

Pike paused here, partly, perhaps, for breath;
partly, certainly, to order his story.

Anthony lit another cigarette. "Other two
men?" he said.

"Right, sir. May as well go on from there as
well as from anywhere. On this second night,
sir, about seven-thirty, Dr. Hale-Storford's outside the house in the garden. That's on the south-
east side of the house, sir, away from that cliff
drop I told you about. He looks down at the
beach—there's a twisty path leads down from
the garden—and he sees a light bobbing about
and hears people talking. He goes down and
sees a boat, half stove in, on the beach. A private boat, sort of little yacht, I make it. This
boat, sir, belongs to a retired naval captain of
the name of Banner—Percy Banner—and it
turns out that he's an old friend of Dr. Hale-
Storford. He's got with him a man much
younger, of the name of Trenchard—Ralph

Trenchard. These gentlemen are soaked through and have got nowhere to go, being about five miles from their home port, which is Fraxton, where Captain Banner lives and this Mr. Trenchard is staying with him.

"Naturally, Dr. Hale-Storford, who, as you may know, sir, is a very friendly, open-hearted sort of a man, takes his old friend Captain Banner and Captain Banner's friend Mr. Trenchard up to the house. They have a hot bath and change of clothes and are asked to stay the night, which they do. After dinner—seems to've been a sort of scratch meal, as you might say, got up by this lady housekeeper, Mrs. Graye—after dinner the whole party sit around for a bit in the drawing room, and then—you must remember, sir, that they've been sort of camping out in this big house and moving furniture here and there and doing all the thousand and one odd jobs there are to do on a big sort of a move like that —the whole party, except Dr. Hale-Storford himself and the two what you might call castaways are so tired that they go to bed. That's about half-past ten, sir."

Anthony interrupted. "Half a minute, Pike! Half a minute! That gives us—let me see—Mrs. Doctor, the Rossiter woman who's Mrs. Doctor's sister; the Andrews—no, Anstruther—boy who's Doctor's cousin; the girl Kerr, who's Mrs. Doctor's friend; and the decayed gentlewoman Graye. They're all in bed by ten-thirty. Hale-Storford, Banner, and Trenchard are downstairs. Right?"

"Yes, sir."

"No one else in the house at all?"

"No, sir."

"No one else been in the house at all that day?"

Pike smiled. "No, sir."

"Sure?"

"Yes, sir."

"And the two dogs. Really loose or shut up in rooms?"

"Really loose, sir. Their beds're in the hall. Right at the back of the hall in a little recess under the stairs. They can hear anything from there. It's been proved."

"And they were all right?"

"Yes, sir."

"That night?"

"Yes, sir."

"Next morning?"

"Yes, sir."

Anthony took out his cigarette case again. "A. R. Gethryn now goes to the foot of the class. Carry on, Pike."

"Well, sir, as you say, the whole party, except those three gentlemen, go upstairs to bed at half-past ten. The three gentlemen stay downstairs. Not in the drawing room now, but in the room that's going to be Dr. Hale-Storford's study. They sit there, smoking and chatting and having a glass of whisky or two, for about an hour and a half. The only one who's any good as to actual time is Captain Banner, and he says that about five minutes before they went upstairs he looked at his watch and saw that it was twenty to twelve. When they do go, Dr. Hale-Storford takes the lamp out of the hall and leads the way upstairs. Everything's quiet upstairs, all doors shut. Leastways, sir, that's according to all three of the gentlemen's stories. Dr. Hale-

Storford leads the way until he gets outside the door of his own room. He stops there and points out to the gentlemen their two doors just close by. While he's talking, Mr. Trenchard suddenly sees what he called 'a dark trickle' coming out from under Dr. Hale-Storford's door. Gave him an awful turn; and Captain Banner, when *he* saw it. Dr. Hale-Storford takes the lamp, opens the door, goes in, and finds Mrs. Hale-Storford, as I told you, sir, on the edge of the bed with her throat cut halfway round. Stone dead. She was half lying on the edge of the bed with her head hanging down so that her hair— only short hair, sir—was on the floor. The blood from her throat had run out, and owing to the lay of the floor—it's a very old house, as I told you—had run right under the door."

Again Anthony interrupted. "Just a minute, Pike. More fathead questions by Carlton Howe. Ready?"

Pike's lantern-shaped and normally lugubrious face split in an enormous grin. "Aye, ready, sir!" he said. "You'll never forget that Carlton Howe, will you?"

"Don't mock, Pike! A great investigator. Probably at his best in the *Case of the Darts of Death*. However, what I want to know is something about these bedrooms. All on the same floor?"

"Yes, sir. Two-storied house. Upstairs, sir, is just what you might call a big gallery round the staircase. Three sides."

"How many rooms?"

Pike did rapid and silent but lip-moving calculations. "Nine bedrooms, sir; one bath; one w. c.; one big storeroom; one what they call still-room; one big linen cupboard, and another they call a cupboard, but which looks more like a spare room to me. That makes fifteen."

"H'm. Give us the order?"

"Easy, sir." Pike took paper and pencil from Lucas's desk and sketched rapidly.

Anthony rose. He looked over Pike's shoulder. When the drawing was done, he took it back to his window seat. He studied it for a moment in silence. He said at last:

"Right. Carry on."

Pike shifted in his chair. He seemed to have

become uneasy. Lucas too grew restless. Pike said:

"That's what happened, sir. Now for the trouble about it! Dr. Hale-Storford, Captain Banner, and Mr. Trenchard say good-night to all the others—Mrs. Hale-Storford included—at half-past ten. And after that *they stay in the study all the time.* Not one of them went out of that room, *at any time for anything,* until they went upstairs and made the discovery. Upstairs, if we leave out the poor lady that was killed, we've got four people. *And nobody else, sir.* And nobody else *could* have got in! And there was no one in that house besides those mentioned. *But* Mrs. Hale-Storford was killed, sir. Murdered. There's no chance of suicide."

"No knife, I suppose?"

"Exactly, sir. And not a trace of one. I've been over that house and over it. And, as you might say, down through it and up through it. I've been into every corner, over every shelf, up every chimney, into every bit of luggage, through every drawer. . . . Everywhere, sir. And when I say everywhere, I mean every-

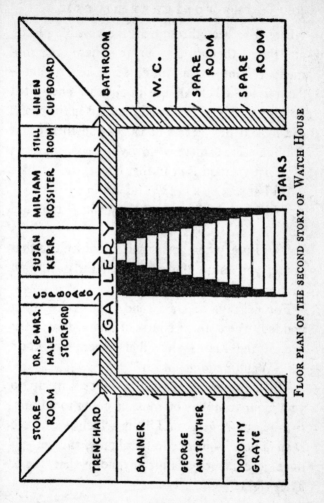

FLOOR PLAN OF THE SECOND STORY OF WATCH HOUSE

where. I've been through all the possible places, and then I thought of you, sir"—here for a moment a faint smile illumined Pike's gloom—"and I looked in all the impossible ones. Still nothing doing." He leaned forward in his chair. He looked first across at Lucas and then up at Anthony. He said very slowly:

"That weapon isn't in that house, sir."

"What sort of a cut?" said Anthony.

"Very, very clean, sir. Very sharp tool did it."

"So, Pike, when you say that tool isn't in that house, you mean that that tool, dirty, isn't in that house."

For perhaps half a second Pike stared, then nodded. "Yes, sir, of course. It could have been one of the razors—but then where are you? . . . Want me to go on, sir?"

"In a minute. Let's see whether I'm up to you. Your trouble, you must be going to tell me, is this: you have got a killing which *must* have been done by someone in that house, and yet you have no evidence against anyone in that house. That right?"

Pike nodded, dolefully grim.

"And of the people in that house it looks more probable that the upstairs bunch contained the killer?"

Pike remonstrated. "More probable, sir? Dead certain, you mean. . . . Unless—unless—oh, gosh! sir, you're not going to say those three gentlemen was all in it together?"

Anthony shrugged. "I'm not saying anything. I'm just trying to take an intelligent interest."

Lucas stared. "What were you thinking of, then?"

"My Creator," said Anthony, "may know. I don't. Just groping, I am. All zeal, Mr. Easy, all zeal! You get me up here, you know, and expect me to listen to these stories and be intelligent. I've got to put up some sort of a show!"

"Oh, shut up!" said Lucas. "Go on, Pike."

Pike looked faint bewilderment. "Where, sir? I mean, what to?"

"You tell *me* something, Pike!" said Anthony. "Let's get rid of facts for a bit. I should say you've had your belly full of 'em. Nasty tricky things, anyhow. Hardly ever spell the truth. Let's have some conjecture."

"Yes, sir." Pike was alert.

"Let's take the case seriatim. Upstairs is more probable. We will start with upstairs. Let's look at this plan of yours a minute. . . . We'll start with Miriam Rossiter."

"Yes, sir."

"What's her age?"

"Forty, sir."

"Look it?"

"No, sir." Pike's head-shake was decisive.

"Good looker?"

Pike was doubtful over this. He said slowly:

"Yes, sir. Has been, very. Dignified type. Tall, very dark. Very reserved kind of lady. One of the sort you think's cold but probably isn't. Just her manner."

"Take this hard?"

"Difficult to say with that type, sir. If you follow me, sir, she's all control, if I can put it that way."

"You can. Relations with Hale-Storford?"

"Very good, I should say, sir. Very good indeed."

"Work? Profession? Hobby?"

"Private means, sir. Seem a fairly well-to-do lot, all of 'em. All of 'em. Don't know about Miss Rossiter's hobbies—not yet, anyhow. Seems to spend seven months out of the year in the south of France and the other five sort of visiting. She's got a little place of her own, sir. Surrey, near Hindhead."

"Right. Next orders, please?"

"Miss Kerr, sir." Pike's previously heavy tone was noticeably lightened, though his face still wore semiofficial immobility. "Young lady, twenty-six. Very neat, sir, very little. What I think you call pettit. Very pretty young lady. Very charming. Lot of pluck too, sir. She seems to have been very fond indeed of the dead lady. They were at school together, and all that. Lot of pluck too, sir. Took it all very quiet."

"Profession? Hobby?"

"Young lady's very well-to-do, sir. Father's Sir David Kerr. Shipping. The young lady, so

I gather, is very what you might call horsey. Hunts most of the winter. Got a lot of horses; goes to all race meetings and that."

"Slangy?" Anthony asked. "Tearaway? 'Huntin', shootin', ridin'—that sort of thing?"

Pike shook his head, firmly. "No, sir, not at all. Know exactly what you mean, but not at all."

"Right. Next, please? That'd be, going right round the corner, the Anstruther boy."

"Quite an ordinary type of lad, sir. Public school, just going up to Cambridge University." Pike seemed inclined to dismiss Mr. Anstruther.

Anthony did not. "Know anything about him, Pike?"

"Everything, sir."

"What's he look like?"

"Biggish. Heavy built but quick on his feet. Very good at games. Played for Somerset, sir, all last season while he was still at school. Captain of football as well. School was Ripton, sir."

"Face?"

Pike stroked his long jaw. "Ordinary sort of

face, sir. Not bad-looking; certainly not handsome."

"Any brains?"

"Oh, yes, sir. Two scholarships to Cambridge University which I take it he didn't want from the money point of view." Pike's voice held a subtle shade of indignation. "Two scholarships at Kyus college, sir."

"H'm! Dressy?"

"Fairly, sir. Not unusually for the age."

"Reactions?"

"Just what you'd expect, sir. Bit dazed at first, then sort of horrified—nearly broke down at the inquest—then, well, I'm not saying anything against the boy, but a bit bored, sort of."

"Quite. Who does he get about with most?"

Pike smiled a small smile. "From what I saw while I was down there, the matter of a week or ten days, he was always *trying* to be with Miss Kerr, and generally *was* with Miss Rossiter."

"H'm! Miss Kerr unkind?"

"No, sir. Not at all, sir. What I mean, though, she naturally didn't want to have this young lad hitched onto her all the time, and

Miss Rossiter didn't mind: she's an older lady.
. . . She was very nice to the boy, I must say
that."

"Right. Let's leave George. Now we come to
our decayed gentlewoman. Is she?"

Again Pike's head-shake was emphatic. "No,
sir, not at all. Very quiet lady, but not the type
you're thinking of. Gives her age as thirty-
seven, but I must say that was a surprise."

"Which way?"

"Right way, sir. Thought she was five or six
years younger than that."

"Reactions?"

"Great shock, sir. Doesn't seem to have quite
the nerves of the other ladies." Pike cut himself short here. His eyes, deliberately blank,
searched Anthony's.

"How great a shock? Prostrate? Bed of sick-
ness? Or walk about tremble-tremble?"

"Both, sir. First two days abed. Tried to get
up, collapsed, and had to go back again."

"Doctor?"

"Dr. Hale-Storford himself, sir. He just gave
her a tonic or some sort of a pick-me-up and

told her to keep in bed. She did, for another day, and then she got up. Didn't seem to me that she ought to have."

"Relations with the others?"

"Very good, sir. They treat her well, she returns it. If you know what I mean, sir, she don't seem to let her—well, it's a sort of servant's work, especially in that house—she don't seem to let it knock her pride about at all. And yet she isn't stiff-necked. . . . Afraid I'm not being very clear on this, sir."

"Lucid, my dear fellow! I could draw you a picture of her. What's she look like?"

"Tall, sir, nearly as tall as Miss Rossiter. Fair colouring. Very—how d'you say?—attractive."

"H'm! Friendly with the boy Anstruther?"

Pike shrugged. "Couldn't say, sir."

There was a long silence. Anthony seemed—as so often he had seemed in this room—rapt in contemplation, apparently painful, of Lucas's steel engravings. Lucas tilted back his chair and lay back, staring at the ceiling. Pike, his head cocked on one side, his long face longer even than its wont, gazed at his boots.

Lucas brought his chair forward with a little crash. He said savagely:

"Well, we're wasting time!"

Anthony looked at him. "My dear fellow! Yes, I see the trouble. Damned nasty case. Somebody must have done it, but who *could* have done it? . . . Coroner's inquest get anywhere?"

"Get anywhere!" Lucas still was savage. "Get anywhere!! Round and round the mulberry bush!"

"Anyone's fault?"

"Oh, damn it! I suppose not! We're doing just the same thing, or Pike has been. No, that's not fair! Sorry, everybody, this thing's got my nerves on edge. Seems so damn ridiculous! Here we've got four possible people who could have done what was done. One or more of 'em must've done it, and yet we can't lay a finger on anybody! . . ."

He got up suddenly and began to walk about the room. Pike and Anthony gazed at him compassionately. As he walked he went on talking. He said:

"D'you mean to tell me, Gethryn, that, though we *know* we've got the people who did it, we can't get anyone?"

"Haven't told you anything," Anthony was smiling. "But if you'd asked me, that's what I might have said. Assuming the continued lack of evidence, what else can you do but nothing? It's only a microcosm of every case."

"How?" The word came from Lucas rather like a bark.

Anthony shrugged. "Well, I ask you! If, when we go out to that lunch I'm going to take you to presently, we find a fat man lying in the middle of the road ripped up the belly, what do we know? We know that his belly's been ripped up by somebody in London. But if you couldn't find that somebody, you wouldn't go about saying it was ridiculous. You'd take it as quite normal. And yet, Lucas, you've got the same position as in this Polferry job. Only in the Polferry job your possibles happen to be four. . . . Or I'd rather call it seven, you know. . . . And in the fat man case you've got somewhere around seven million."

Pike laughed; then immediately controlled himself, darting a look of apology at Lucas.

Lucas glared at Anthony. "All very well! Damn clever and all that, and I see what you mean. But you're not being helpful, exactly, are you?"

"My dear fellow! Helpful? You tell me here's a case that nobody can help in, and then you accuse me of not being helpful. . . . There's just two courses for you to follow, Lucas. The first is: Take a fresh piece of paper and do it all over again. That's long and difficult and may get you the same answer. The second and wisest is to call it a miss."

Lucas exploded. "Call it a miss! How the hell can we call it a miss? There's a woman killed. There's four people, one of whom must have done it. Four people and we can't get one. Call it a miss!"

Anthony stood up. "Thinking of Justice, are you? Or a second leader in the *Daily Express?*"

"Both! Both!" Lucas stopped in his walk. He faced Anthony. He said, after a pause:

"Look here, Gethryn! . . ." There was a note of excitement in his voice.

Anthony shook his head. "No. No. Sorry. But the Gethryn family really is off to look for air . . . and anyhow, you know, I shouldn't make any better fist of it than Pike."

For a moment a smile twisted Pike's long face, but it was gone as soon as it had come. He shook his head. "No, sir. That won't do. Remember the Hoode case. Remember the Lines-Bower case. Remember Bronson. . . . You can't remember all those, sir, and then think that you mightn't be able to . . ."

Anthony raised a hand. "It's no good, Pike. I'll say the same to you as I did to Mr. Lucas. The Gethryn family are going for air. You've told me all about it, with the result that I, just like you, know nothing. . . . Leave it alone, Lucas. Leave it alone!"

Lucas stood leaning his arms upon the back of his chair. He said:

"My good Gethryn! How the devil *can* we leave it alone? There you've got——"

"Oh! Please!" Anthony's tone was compelling. "Come out to lunch now. Come to Marvel's. I'll give you something to put in your tummy that'll make you forget all about it. Not your tummy, the Polferry riddle. Good title that! Come on out!"

Lucas stood irresolute. Pike rose. Pike went to Anthony. Pike said, in a low and penetrating whisper:

"All very well, sir, but Mr. Lucas is right. Here we are. The C. I. D. We've been called in to make something out of this tangle and we've *got* to make something out of it." His lean face was doleful, but there was a great eagerness in his eyes. "It's like this: It wouldn't matter so much if this could possibly've been an outside job. If it could've been, we might've been able to cook up the usual stuff and nobody could say much to us if we didn't get any forrader. But it couldn't have been an outside job, and the public *knows* it couldn't have been an outside job, and the public *knows*—you may not read the papers, sir, but I assure you there's been a great deal about this case in 'em—and the public *knows* that not only was it an inside

job but that there were only four people who
could be expected to include the murderer. . . .
Now, if you . . ."

Anthony shook his head. "It's no good, Pike.
Not a bit. The Gethryn family, as I seem to
have remarked somewhere before, are depart-
ing from this island at once."

Lucas straightened himself; walked to his
cupboard and took out coat and hat and stick.
With these in his arms he turned. He said to
Anthony:

"Mean that?"

Anthony nodded. "Every word of it. . . .
Sorry. The best thing you can do with that job
is to put it on one side. . . . It's not a murder,
you know. Not at all. More like a penny-in-the-
slot 'Spot the Winner.' "

Lucas struggled slowly into his coat. He said:

"Did you say anything about lunch?"

Again Anthony nodded. "I did, but I'm dou-
ble damned if I'll take you if you're going to
talk Polferry all the time. Hands off Polferry!
Coming?"

Lucas picked up his stick. "Oh, I suppose so. . . . All right, Pike. Let's forget it."

"Forget it, sir?" Pike was incredulous.

"Until," said Lucas, "half-past four this afternoon. You'd better come and see me again then, and we'll both go along to the Commissioner."

Pike's lower jaw thrust itself out until it became almost a deformity. He looked at Anthony. He said:

"Isn't there a chance, sir?"

Anthony shook his head, smiling. "Nary chance, Pike. Nary chance. As I've told you once, this sort of job is your sort of job. There's no man anywhere who can touch you at it. You carry on with it. Sooner or later you'll get something. If anyone can, *you* can."

Pike smiled without noticeably lessening his gloom. "Butter's all very well, sir. Very nice on bread and all that."

Anthony grinned. "I know. I know. But I meant what I said. Carry on. Good-bye, Pike, and good luck! Drop me a line and let me know how the show goes on. Funny business, you know. . . . Come on, Lucas!"

Lucas went, and the door closed behind them.

Pike was left staring at its inner side. His lips moved soundlessly.

CHAPTER THREE

ANTHONY was eating marrons glacés. He was also, most unusually, reading an English newspaper. The sky was impossibly blue. The snow upon the slopes of the Roche Menon across the valley was incredibly white. Into the revolving wooden sun house in which he sat the sun streamed; the Swiss sun whose heat is so often in such paradoxical contrast to the thermometer. He turned over the pages of the paper idly. It was an *Evening Planet,* three weeks old. Up the steep narrow path from the chalet came Lucia Gethryn—a white-clad figure of grace and beauty and health. She sat beside him on the wooden bench. She looked at the half-empty box of sweetmeats. She said:

"Pig! Oh, pig! One, two, three . . ."

"More, probably," said her husband. "Have one?"

Lucia nibbled. She glanced down at the paper on his knees. She said:

"Aren't you well, dear?"

Anthony began to fold the paper. "Eminently. What's fit for you to read . . . Great Scott!"

Lucia turned to stare at him. She knew that tone. He had unfolded the paper again and now read in silence. It seemed many minutes before he set the sheets down upon the bench beside him and rose. He stretched himself then. He murmured something and was gone. After him Lucia called:

"Where're you going?"

He turned in the path. "Telephone. Back in a moment."

Lucia sat looking out across the valley at the dazzling whiteness of the snow slopes. The glare hurt her eyes; she turned her head away, and her glance fell upon the folded paper. She picked it up. There was the paragraph which

he had been reading. She read too. She
read:

BOY CRICKETER DROWNED

Tragic Fate of George Anstruther

DOCTOR'S GALLANT ATTEMPT FRUITLESS

Chain of Tragedy

(*From the* PLANET'S *special correspondent*)

Polferry, Wessex.

AT THREE o'clock yesterday afternoon a boating
tragedy occurred here, when Mr. George Anstruther, the well known young cricketer, was drowned
within sight of the beach jetty.

A most gallant attempt to rescue his young cousin was made by Dr. Richard Hale-Storford, the
famous cancer research surgeon. When the accident
which led to his death occurred Mr. Anstruther
was sailing Dr. Storford's yawl *Bluebird*. He
was alone in the boat and had just set out from the
jetty. Fishermen and others on the jetty suddenly
noticed that the boat was about to founder; it was
labouring and apparently half filled with water.
They could see young Mr. Anstruther bailing
desperately. By an evil chance there were no

other craft of any kind available. Two fishermen, Bert Dawling and Albert Tresidder, immediately set off for the next point about a mile along the shore to where a boat could be obtained. The *Bluebird* suddenly keeled over, and the remaining horrified spectators saw Mr. Anstruther disappear. He came up again, however, and started to strike out for the shore, being then nearly a quarter of a mile out. Unfortunately the tide was against him.

Dr. Hale-Storford, with whom Mr. Anstruther had been staying, had in the meantime arrived upon the scene. Seeing that there was no boat yet available in which to go out to help and knowing that his young cousin was far from being a strong swimmer, he stripped off his outer clothing immediately and dived from the jetty. Dr. Hale-Storford himself is a very strong swimmer. Helped by the tide, he made rapid progress, but the onlookers were horrified to see that, when quite a distance still separated the two, Mr. Anstruther was visibly weakening. He then, when Dr. Hale-Storford was about fifty yards from him, sank, but came up again to continue his battling when the doctor was twenty-five yards nearer. Just before he sank for the second time, Dr. Hale-Storford came up with him and

clutched at him. The spectators were greatly heart-
ened at this, as they thought that Mr. Anstruther
was allowing Dr. Hale-Storford to tow him in the
approved manner, and further hope was given to
them when a motor launch was seen some way off
hurrying toward the swimmers. Dr. Hale-Storford
did not at first see the motorboat. He struggled
gamely on. When he did sight it, he slackened his
efforts and contented himself with supporting his
cousin. When the motorboat drew level with the
swimmers and dragged them aboard, however, it
was found that Mr. Anstruther was beyond recall.

Great Loss

Cricket enthusiasts will be particularly aghast at
the tragedy. Mr. Anstruther, who played all last
season, when he was still at Ripton School, for his
county, was one of the most promising young bats in
the country. He was to proceed after Christmas to
Cambridge University, where he was certain of getting his Blue. Besides being an all-round sportsman,
he was a young man of brains, and his loss will be
felt deeply by his many friends. He had few relations, his father and mother, Sir William Anstruther and Lady Anstruther, having died ten years
ago. Mr. George Anstruther lived with a guardian,
Mr. Hastings Pollock, of The Grange, Bury-St.-

Wilfred, Kent. He was spending a long vacation, however, with his cousin, Dr. Hale-Storford.

Doctor's Outburst

"Fate must owe me a grudge." These words, spoken in a tone of controlled but indescribable bitterness and pain, burst from Dr. Hale-Storford when he found that, despite all his gallant efforts, his young cousin was dead. Readers will remember that it is less than seven months since Dr. Hale-Storford lost his wife under the most mysterious and astonishing circumstances, and that less than two months ago, Miss Miriam Rossiter, his sister-in-law, was killed in a motoring accident on Polferry Hill.

Lucia finished her reading. There came to her ears the sound of her husband's step, and then his entrance, momentarily blocking the flood of sunshine. She set the paper down. He came and sat beside her. She slipped her hand through his arm and said:

"What's all the telephoning?"

"Just a craving for journalism." Anthony was vague. "All I did was to ring up Stein at the hotel. Asked him whether he could rake up some old papers for me. He could. What're you doing this afternoon?"

Lucia's eyes travelled from her husband's face to the discarded paper, then back again. She opened her mouth to speak, but changed her mind. She got up.

"Tennis, I suppose," she said. "Will you?"

He shook his head. "Not if you can do without me. . . . Let's go and see Alan. Where is he?"

"Out at the back of the chalet with Nannie. Let's."

Arm in arm they went down the narrow path. At the bottom, just as they were turning into the wider sweep which ran round the chalet to the terraced garden at its rear, Lucia halted. Anthony, checked by the hand through his arm, halted too. She looked up at him. His gaze was abstract. He was looking out across the valley to the Roche Menon, but it was plain he saw neither snow nor mountains nor valley. The fingers squeezed his arm.

"Oyster!" said Lucia. "You *might* talk, but I suppose you won't, not until you're . . ."

"Talk!" Anthony, without moving, gave the impression of a man who has just shaken himself. "Talk! You wait, my woman! Come on, where's this kid?"

(2)

The large and flat and orange-coloured envelope addressed in the angular writing of his good friend M. Stein lay beside Anthony's breakfast plate three mornings later. He made no parade of his interest in it, but it is to be noted that well within an hour he was once more in the little sun house, and once more reading a paper and an English paper. This time it was *The Courier;* date, November 21st of the previous year. He did not have far to look for what he wanted. It was splashed about the front page. The headlines were in even more excitable type than that common to *Courier* headlines.

He read once, and then again. After the second reading he let the paper slip from his hands. It sprawled untidy and unheeded by his feet. He smoked one pipe and then another. He did not seem to hear Lucia's approach. She was, before he looked up, actually within the hut. She sat down beside him, stooped, and picked up the crumpled sheets. She straightened them, smoothed out the front one, and glanced at the headlines. She said:

"I thought so. But why's it worry you?"

Anthony looked at her. "Who's worried?"

"Don't be silly! *You* are. At least, something's on your mind. Ever since you were reading that paper in here the other day—that other paper—you've been miles away somewhere. You haven't written a word. You haven't played any tennis. You *have* been fit to speak to, because, strangely enough, you nearly always are, but to try and sit there and tell me there's nothing on your mind—that's just silly. Especially as I know what it is."

"You know, do you?" He looked at her again. A little smile twisted one corner of his mouth. "Yes, I s'pose you do. What is it?"

Lucia tapped the paper impatiently. "This, of course!"

"What? Lord Otterbourn?"

"Don't be *exasperating!* No, this—*this!* This—what's the man's name?—Hale-Storford business. What I want to know is, *why?*"

Anthony's smile became a grin. "So do I. We must've both got to the same stage."

He became aware that Lucia was, with calculating wrath, eyeing him up and down. He shifted nervously. He said:

"All right! All right! I'll be good! What d'you want me to do?"

"Tell me all about it."

"That, my dear, is not at all a sensible thing to say. If I knew all about it I shouldn't be what you call worried. It's because I know nothing at all about it that I'm what you call worried."

"Just one more bit of rubbish like that," Lucia said, "and I shall fall upon you. I know you're cursing me for being a nuisance, but I don't mind."

Anthony grinned. "All right, all right! I don't think I told you, but just before we left I saw Lucas. Now, he was worried, very. About the Hale-Storford case. And I must say with some reason."

"You mean because it looked as if they must be able to find out who killed the poor man's wife and yet they couldn't?"

"Exactly, Lecoq! I pointed out to him that logically he oughtn't to be worried over that more than any——"

"You would! I don't suppose that made him stop worrying, but I do suppose he asked you to stay and help."

Anthony nodded. "I couldn't, though. Anyhow, what could I have done? Pike had been on the job, and Pike, as you know, is a very good man. . . . No, I forgot all about it, except in the way of an occasional and very passing thought. But I remembered all about it when I was reading that paper the other day. Did you see that paper? Did you see that the boy Anstruther—who was one of the people staying in the house when the Hale-Storford woman was killed—had been drowned?"

It was Lucia's turn to nod.

"And did you see at the end of the account

of that drowning that this was the second death, within about six months, of members of that original house party?"

Lucia stared. "No, I didn't." She glanced down at the paper she still held. "Oh, I see. . . ."

"Exactly. Three months before Mr. Anstruther gets drowned, Miss Rossiter gets broken to pieces. Hence all this chain-of-tragedy, Fate's-hand sort of thing. . . . What're you doing?"

Lucia's head was bent over the paper. "Reading." She read. She lifted her head again at last. She said:

"You may not like the way they put it, but surely 'Fate takes a hand' is about right. . . . What did they say at the end of the inquest, by the way?—about poor Mrs. Hale-Storford?"

"What they said at the end of the inquest about poor Mrs. Hale-Storford was that poor Mrs. Hale-Storford had been killed by a person or persons unknown. Not very original."

Lucia pondered. "But surely—surely there was something about a tramp?"

"My dear child, when a coroner or a coroner's jury don't know what to say they always say something about a tramp. Here you have what amounted to an impossibility of the woman's death having been caused by anyone *outside* the house. But they couldn't prove that death had been caused by anyone *inside* the house. Hence your tramp . . ." His voice died away. He bent down to knock the ashes from his pipe.

The sun was streaming fully into the hut, but Lucia suddenly shivered.

"Cold, dear?" said her husband.

"N-no. Somebody walking over my grave. . . . I was just thinking, how terrible for the husband."

Anthony shrugged. "What about the other people who were in the house and who *didn't* do it?"

Lucia held out her hand. "Give me a cigarette, will you? And then start at the beginning."

Anthony gave her the cigarette, held a match to it, said, when it was glowing:

"P'r'aps you're right. . . . On the fifteenth of September, Hale-Storford, his wife, his wife's sister, his wife's friend, his own young male cousin, and his housekeeper move into the Watch House, which overlooks the mouth of the Starr estuary. There are these six people only in the house. There are no servants, and will not be any until the following week. On the sixteenth of September, tired after a day's furniture shifting, the young male cousin, the wife, the wife's sister, wife's friend, and the housekeeper go to bed at 10:30 P. M. Each has a different room. Downstairs Hale-Storford and two stranded friends, a retired naval captain named Banner, and an indeterminate fellow named Trenchard, stay to smoke and drink and talk. The house is locked up. There are two enormous dogs loose in the house, very good watchdogs. It is a foul night. The house is inaccessible except on one side. Probably—almost certainly—no outsider could have got into the house, killed the woman, and got out of the house again.

"Hale-Storford and his two friends go up to bed at about a quarter to twelve. They've been in that room, together. No one of them, say the other two, has left that room since ten-thirty, when the first party went bedward. On getting upstairs they find that Eve Hale-Storford has had her throat cut and has bled to death. The doctors fix the death as having taken place somewhere between ten-thirty and eleven forty-five, which is very, very clever of them. Immediately after the discovery Hale-Storford sends Trenchard downstairs to telephone for the police, and, with Banner, goes round to each of the other occupied rooms. In every case the occupant is either asleep or pretending to be asleep and has to be roused. All are aghast. At the subsequent inquest not even the more nosey questioning nor the concurrent efforts of the police can unearth the slightest reason for any of those persons within the house—including even the apparently impossible suspects, Hale-Storford himself, Banner and Trenchard—wishing to kill Mrs. Hale-Storford. Mrs. Hale-Storford can't have killed herself, for no trace can be found of the weapon which killed her. Verdict of coroner's jury—person or persons unknown, which equals one convenient tramp.

"We are left, then, with four unarrestable *possibles*—the boy Anstruther, the housekeeper Mrs. Graye, the sister Miriam Rossiter, the friend Susan Kerr. We also have three unarrestable *unlikelys*—Hale-Storford himself, Banner, and Trenchard."

"But they aren't *unlikelys*, surely? They must be *impossibles*."

Anthony looked at her with large grave eyes of sorrow. "Oh, my dear—and oh!"

"But you said just now that those three people were downstairs together all the time and that none of them left the room. Therefore they——"

"My dear Lucia, you're losing your grip, your touch! Those three can't qualify for the *impossible* class. We've only their word for it that none of them left the room."

"You mean that they might *all* . . ." Lucia's face had grown suddenly white.

"Exactly. Unlikely, but not impossible."

"Well, I don't care *what* you say. *I* think it's impossible."

"What you really mean," Anthony said, "is

that it is very, very improbable. . . . Now don't speak, I'm going on. We get left with— let me see— as far as I see at present, five distinct possibilities. I'll write them down." He took a notebook from his pocket, tore out a page, and wrote rapidly.

Lucia's eyes followed the flying pencil. She read:

POSSIBILITIES

UPSTAIRS PARTY	(1)	That the murder was done by one of the upstairs party *with the knowledge of no one else at all.* 100.
	(2)	That the murder was done by one of the upstairs party *with the knowledge of some other person or persons within the house.* 50.
DOWNSTAIRS PARTY	(3)	That the murder was done by one of the downstairs party with the knowledge at least of both the others in that party. 25.
OUTSIDE	(4)	That the murder was done by an outsider entering and leaving the house *without the knowledge of anyone within the house.* NIL.

DOWNSTAIRS, UPSTAIRS, OUTSIDE PARTIES	(5) That the murder was done by an outsider entering and leaving the house *with the connivance of someone or ones inside the house.* 10.
SUICIDE	(6) That the killing was done by Eve Hale-Storford herself and that an outsider removed the weapon. NIL.
	(7) That the killing was done by Eve Hale-Storford herself and that someone within the house removed the weapon. 25.

Underneath the seventh point, the pencil drew the flourish of finality. Anthony held out the little sheet. Lucia took it and read again. When she raised her head it was to find her husband looking at her with the small smile which she knew so well. She said, giving back the paper:

"Yes. But aren't some of these—well—almost impossibilities?"

Anthony nodded. "Observe the figures against each point. They're probability marks on a percentage basis. First we have murder being done by one of the upstairs party entirely

on his or her own, 100. (2), The murder being
done by one of the upstairs party not on his or
her own, 50. I think we can assume that the
likelihood of a job of that kind being worked
out by two people of that kind is only half. Now,
(3), that the murder was done by one of the
downstairs lot, who *must* have had—because
they all backed each other up in their alibis—
the knowledge of the other two. Well, I don't
think that's worth more than 25. (4), The "lone-
hand" outsider. No marks at all. The inacces-
sibility of the house; the presence of the dogs;
the intense improbability of premeditation, and
the reputed locking up of the house—all these
together fairly reduce this fellow's marks to
nothing. Then (5). The outsider helped by the
insider. I have given him 10. Then (6). Suicide
plus an outsider. I've put down nil, but I think
I ought to have put minus nil. (7), though, is a
different matter. You may think 25 is too much.
But I think it must be 25 until we know, if ever
we do, a great deal more about the dramatis
personæ. . . . Have you got all this? Don't forget you asked me for it. . . . Right. . . . We now

pass on to a survey of the events of the next seven months. Now, seven months is not a long time, whichever way you look at it. Yet in seven months there die violent deaths no fewer than two of our unarrestable possibles. The first is Miriam Rossiter, the murdered woman's sister. She is driving down from the top of Polferry Hill, which is by hundreds of feet the highest part of that part of the Wessex coast. Her car swerves or skids or—something, and she goes over the edge, and that's that. It's at night, there's no one about, and she's not found until next morning. That's on the twenty-first of November.

"Four months later, an even shorter time you will notice, Watson, than the seven months I spoke of just now, young Anstruther gets drowned. He is out sailing when——"

Lucia laid her hand on his shoulder. "Yes, yes. I read all that in that paper. What I *don't* see, what I *can't* see, is how it joins on, *really,* to Mrs. Hale-Storford. The poor woman gets killed and nobody knows who did it. That's beastly, but it's not absolutely unusual, is it?

And then two of the people who might have been the people who did it get killed too. But they're killed in the way hundreds of people are killed every day. Horrible, I know, but as I see it—— Anthony! You're not going to tell me that you think they're the people who did it and that they—that they——"

She broke off. She seemed at a loss for words, but her eyes searched her husband's face. Anthony smiled.

"Surely! Who's getting mixed now? What are *you* trying to say?"

There came an answering smile, but the dark eyes were troubled still. "I don't know," she said. "You tell me!"

"At the moment you're just being another of the 'chain-of-tragedy, hand-of-faters'; in fact, you looked quite scared at the sudden thought that a Conan-Doyle Nemesis may have overtaken two villains. That's what you're thinking. I'm not . . ."

Silence. Lucia waited. Still silence. She was looking down at the old copy of *The Courier*, now twisted into a tight roll between her fingers. When she did look at her husband she saw that he was once more placidly smoking. She threw the paper down. She said with a little rush of words:

"You *are* irritating! Go on! Go on!"

Anthony took the pipe out of his mouth and smiled at her. "Sorry, dear! You know I don't mean to get like this, but I can't help it. What you want me to tell you is what I'm thinking, but I can't, because I don't know. Now, now, that's not clever, it's purely a statement of fact. We've been married quite long enough for you to know me by this time, but you never seem to have understood properly what a tidy mind I've got. That, you know, is really why I'm always getting mixed up in this 'finding-out' business. When I see a thing all unreasonable and all at loose ends, I just have to see whether I can't straighten it out, and it's the same with my own thinking. When my own thinking's just a mess, it isn't tidy, and therefore I won't let it release its untidiness onto the world. I have to get it nicely rearranged and sorted before I can really talk."

Lucia smiled at him. She shifted a little closer along the seat and slid her hand through his arm.

"Even to me?" she said.

Anthony laughed. "Damn you!" he said. "Oh, damn you! I can't tell you what I'm thinking. I don't know what I'm thinking. . . . Look here. The farthest I'll go is to say this. The whole Hale-Storford job's so messy that there must be something wrong with it. There's an original murder. That, because it's been impossible to fix upon anybody, has got eight loose ends to it; if you found one the right one and put a rope round it and pulled it, all the others would jump back properly into their places. But as it is, they're just—eight of 'em—all waving about messily in the breeze. Or all *were* waving messily about in the breeze. Now, two of those loose ends have been cut off. They haven't been cut off tidily. They've been cut off clumsily, so that their jagged remains are untidier than ever. Get me?"

"Yes! Yes! Go on."

"I won't go on because I can't. . . . Tell you

what I'll do, though. To-morrow, no, the next day, when I get an answer to a letter I wrote the day before yesterday, I'll talk to you some more. That talk may be to say that there's nothing more doing on the subject, or it may be to say that there is. I can't tell. If I promise that, will you shut up? Can we go and play tennis or something?"

The arm linked in his arm pressed gently. "Yes, I'll agree to that, dear. If . . ."

"If what?"

He tried to look down at her face but could see only the top of her dark head.

"If," said a small voice, "you'll tell me just two more things." The words were slightly muffled. She was laughing.

"Go on, then. P'r'aps I will, p'r'aps I won't. What are they?"

"First, d'you know how Dr. Hale-Storford took this horrible tragedy of his wife's death? Second—I haven't read all that—was that motor accident that killed Miss What's-her-name— Rossiter—a likely motor accident?"

Anthony disengaged his arm. He stood up, looking at his watch. He said:

"It's now two minutes to eleven. After eleven this subject is closed until that letter. First answer, Hale-Storford was as near broken as a good man can be. Second answer, couldn't say until after that letter. Come on, now!"

CHAPTER FOUR

THE long blue Bentley coupé of Miss Susan
Kerr pulled up at that corner of the Row which
faces the gates at Hyde Park Corner. An im-
pressive car. The loiterers looked at it with
mouths slightly more open even than usual.
They also gaped, when she got down, at Miss
Kerr herself.

Miss Kerr was very small and extremely
neat. Her face, when one was near enough properly to see it, more than bore out the promises
made by the rest of her. It, too, was small; it,
too, was neat; but there was about its very neat-
ness a certain most charming irregularity which
had always saved it from the stigma of pretti-
ness.

Miss Kerr, this morning, as upon every
morning anywhere at this time, was about to
ride. She left the Bentley to its own immovable
and superior devices and with neat, swift,

strides crossed the gravel path and came onto
the tan itself. Just by that point where ends the
railing which divides the tan from the footpath
upon the roadway side was an old and smart
and saturnine groom, holding a big bay mare
whose every restless but utterly graceful movement, whose every line and every vein told of
her breeding. About the railings by this horse
was another group of loiterers, also with
mouths slightly more agape than usual. This
horse of Miss Kerr's, like Miss Kerr's self,
seemed even to their untutored eyes very different matter from the Row's usual offerings.

Miss Kerr smiled at her groom. Her groom
saluted Miss Kerr. She walked round the mare,
surveying her. She gave a little nod as if of
approval.

"Looks well, doesn't she?" she said.

The old groom began to blow. His words,
when he spoke, seemed to come out as merely
part and parcel of a steady hissing. He said:

"Looks well enough. 'Orrible 'andful this
mornin', though, Miss. Fair rattled me old
bones up gettin' 'er 'ere."

"Don't be an old pessimist, George." Miss Kerr took the reins in her left hand, a grip of saddle with her right, and lifted the left of those admirable boots.

George, with deftness, put her up. The bay mare snorted; danced; made those little ominous back-to-front rocking movements which are often the prelude to real "standing-up." George caught at her head.

"Stand there!" said George. He also said, fortunately not quite audibly, a great deal more.

Susan laughed. "You let go of her head, George. Go on. Do as I tell you."

George, with reluctance, did as he was bid. George also made a remark which apparently had to do with the highly qualified foolishness of some people in bringing such even more highly qualified horses to such an inaudibly unpleasant place as London.

Susan's hands with a horse were the envy of a great part of Leicestershire and many, many show rings. She checked that tendency for biped progression. She put the mare to a walk. She called over her shoulder:

"George, go and sit in the car and smoke yourself into a good temper. I'm only going twice round."

She did not go once round.

Down the Row, toward Knightsbridge barracks, she rode. First, while the mare showed tendency to dance which must be repressed, at a walk, and then, when, with movement, the mare quietened, at a trot.

About fifty yards before that break in the railings which is opposite the first gate after Hyde Park Corner, a small car backfired. Any excuse, thought the bay, is better than none. She put her ears flat and flung up her heels. She tried—very hard she tried—to get that pretty, wicked-eyed head right down, but she couldn't. Those hands which seemed like feathers could also be strong as iron. Susan laughed. To her a horse wasn't much good if it didn't need riding. There was a little scurry while the argument went on. Tan flew. And then the plunging attempts to start a tear-away gallop were subdued. The mare pranced, but she pranced straightforward and orderly. Susan, her cheeks a shade pinker, her smile serene, looked about. She was now abreast of that break in the railings and consequently the gate across the road. She waved to a girl of her acquaintance and received an answering wave. She began to cross the gap. There was a little line of cars abreast of her, held up by the traffic policeman. The exhaust of one was roaring. The mare's ears began to flatten. Susan bent forward to gentle the arched neck—and then it happened.

There is a great difference in feeling—any horseman will tell you—between that of a horse who *may* catch hold and go with you and that of a horse who *has* caught hold and is going to go with you whatever you do. Susan had the second of these two feelings, and it is a feeling whose unpleasantness increases in direct ratio with the rider's skill and experience. Susan didn't like it at all. Susan, quite frankly, was scared. The mare had both bits well between her teeth; her neck and head were straight out in one continuous line; she was going like the wind. By the wild, uncontrolled speed of her it was plain that for the while, at least, she ran

without sense. Something—something quite unusual—had startled her. She had gone off almost as if she had been struck unexpectedly. . . .
But Susan was not thinking of any of these
things. Susan was occupied with wondering
solely what was going to happen to Susan. She
did what she could, which was practically nothing. The wind of their going caught at her. It
seemed to pour itself down her throat until it
was impossible almost for her to breathe. . . .

Vaguely she heard shoutings. Vaguely she
saw, streaming past, with the roadway and the
trees, white-faced scurrying people; other people, motionless, agape; others who made futile
movements as if to check her flight.

Now she was almost at the curve at the Serpentine end. . . . She was round the curve. Her
breath was almost gone; her arms merely an
ache. . . .

And then that heaven-sent riding master—
Mr. James Tunkin—with his own gray cob and
no fewer than four empty-saddled ponies,
whose riders were now on their way home. Mr.
Tunkin saw her coming. Mr. Tunkin saw what

he might do with a bit of luck and, like the good
fellow he was, promptly tried to do it. Tried and
succeeded. He spurred the old cob into the very
centre of the way. The cob snorted. It could
hear the thunder of hoofs and could see whence
that thunder was coming. The ponies, as Mr.
Tunkin had hoped they might, fanned out in a
jiffling, terrorized fan. He managed—quite
how, he doesn't know to this day—to keep his
hold upon their leading reins. For just the one
necessary moment, Mr. Tunkin, his cob, and
the four ponies blocked the Row from rail to
rail. No more than any other horse who is not
actually insane would Susan's bay mare over-
ride either another horse or a man. Up to the
very last moment she kept up her stampede. But
at that last moment she checked, throwing out
stiff before her her beautiful fore legs, drag-
ging after them the down-curved hinds. With
a slithering rush she came to a halt and at the
moment of actually halting had perforce to re-
arrange her balance so that now her outthrust
head was in the tan and the weight of her
borne fully upon the shoulders. . . .

Susan, her legs without power to grip, her head whirling, her breath gone, tumbled forward and over. She landed sitting. She was right between the forefeet of Mr. Tunkin's gray. She said afterward that the first thing she really remembered after the start of that bolt was sitting there and looking up at two faces. One a frightened gray equine face, and the other an astonished brown human face.

"Gord save us all!" said Mr. Tunkin.

Susan fought for her breath. Before she had quite got it she smiled at the two faces. She said:

"He seems . . . to have . . . had . . . a pretty good . . . try." And then she began to laugh.

"Gord stiffen me!" said Mr. Tunkin.

Somehow he scrambled off the cob. Somehow collected all those myriad reins into one hand. Somehow stretched out his other hand and pulled Susan to her feet.

At that moment Mr. Tunkin's fortune was made. Within three years he had almost forgotten those lean times when he had been merely a struggling Bayswater jobmaster.

Susan never forgot her friends any more than they forgot Susan.

She did not say much to Mr. Tunkin then. Still holding his hand, she stood up, struggling for breath. And then, with a heart-catching banging of clutch and screaming of brakes, the Bentley drew up beside the rails. It was not on the road. It was on the path. One of its just now beautifully flared black wings looked like part of a discarded perambulator.

"George!" cried Susan.

George, despite his sixty years, was already out of the car and over the rails. As he came there issued from his lips a sound like many kettles all boiling.

"George," said Susan, "I didn't know you could drive the car."

George hissed. "Can't," said George, "and 'ow many times 'ave I told you that it's sheer bloody foolery to bring a bloody horse like this to a bloody place like bloody London. That's the worst of you bloody kids. You never know when to bloody well stop. The bloody thing might 'a' broke your bloody neck *and* 'er own—

not but what that last wouldn't 'ave been a good job. Look at her now, standing there looking as though butter wouldn't melt in her bloody mouth."

"Now then," said Mr. Tunkin at last, "language."

Susan reeled; clutched at the railings. George leaped for her, but checked his leap when he saw that the stagger's cause was laughter.

He walked off to where the bay mare, now placid, was nearly staking herself in an endeavor to reach the rhododendron leaves.

(2)

Bird, who was the butler of Sir David Kerr, closed the door of the library behind him with even more than his usual softness. A small frown of bewilderment creased the expansive and usually placid brow. At the foot of the stairs he saw coming down them Hewson, who was Sir David Kerr's valet. When their heads were level Hewson said:

"Get anything?" His voice was the trained

non-carrying subtone of the experienced servant.

Bird shook his bald head. The frown increased. "Don't know what's up with him. Walking about up and down in there like a caged animal. Really wild, Hewson, white of the eye and all that. Hardly seemed to know I was there, if you know what I mean. And when I did cough and ask him whether he'd like a drink and then tried to get the usual out of him, all I got was: 'Don't talk to me about *horses*.' It wasn't the words so much as the way he said 'em. You'd 'ave thought, m' lad, that in spite of horses being, so to say, his religion and his work, they was his Annie Themer."

"Who's that?" said Hewson.

"A word, Hewson"—Bird was all benevolent superiority—"meanin' a thing that you can't abide more than anything else."

Hewson whistled. "Said that about horses, did he? . . . Oh! *I* know! Did he go round to the mews before he came here?"

Bird nodded gravely. "Why?"

" 'E's been talkin' to George, that's what it is.

I saw George for a minute just now when he brought the horse back. That new one. 'E muttered something about her having 'ad a spill or something."

"That's it, then." Bird's tone was no longer bewildered. "I'll try to catch 'im before 'e goes out. 'E'll be all right after a couple of hours, when *she's* down. I did want to know about that Guiding Star. If you look at the weight, Hewson, that horse has got to carry, and him only the age he is, I don't see——"

"Bill-oh!" said Hewson out of the corner of his mouth.

Bird bill-ohed. He proceeded up the stairs with massive dignity. On the landing he stood aside with grave humility while Susan brushed by. He must have caught something of her smile, for he, too, was smiling when he went on his way.

Trevor Heath, once a Squadron Leader in the Black Huzzars, now the second most successful trainer and steeplechase rider in England, was still prowling up and down the library of his future father-in-law's house.

The hearth was littered with cigarettes which he had lighted only to throw them away so soon as he found them in his mouth. His thin, clean-shaven face was of a curious gray pallor; there was no blood beneath the tan; a deep frown pulled together the fair brows over the rather deep-set blue eyes. It was not like this that he generally waited in this room. . . .

The door burst open; was slammed again. Inside it stood Susan. Susan very small, and Susan very neat. A Susan, in fact, against whom it seemed impossible to harden one's heart.

Generally, upon these rare mornings when Trevor got up to town so early, their common delight at the gift of an extra few hours together made their meeting place within this room less than three feet from the door. But to-day Trevor stood his ground. Susan checked in her advance; stood herself.

"Trevor!" said Susan.

He threw away the fourteenth untasted cigarette. He thrust his hands deep into his trousers pockets. His mouth was a hard thin line. He did not move. He looked at her.

"Trevor!" said Susan again. She came forward slowly.

He stood his ground. She came up to him. He had his back to the room's one window, and his face was in shadow. She peered at it.

"Trevor!" she said for the third time. Then: "What's the matter, dear?"

He moved now. He took his hands from his pockets. He took her by the shoulders and gently thrust her into a chair; went back to the fireplace; stood, his hands behind his back, his back itself against the mantelpiece, still staring at her. He said:

"I've been talking to George."

Susan was out of her chair and close to him in one movement. Her face, whose pallor for these last few moments had almost matched the man's, was her own again and smiling. She put up her hands and took between the fingers and thumb of each a lapel of his coat. She said:

"Trevor darling! . . . That's what it was! You are a devil, you frightened me! I thought it was something really wrong."

He exploded at that. "Really wrong!" he said

without opening his teeth. "Susan, will you go and sit down!"

The smile left her face. She was grave again, but the twitching of her lips belied her. With an assumed meekness quite wholly delightful she went back to her chair. She sat in it very straight and prim, her hands folded in her lap. She looked like a patient schoolgirl waiting for a necessary but harmless lecture from a parent doting but duty bound.

There was silence. Heath, his face still set, and with none of the colour back in it, looked at her. Susan waited. Still silence. At last she said, in a voice very small:

"I've sat down, Trevor. Can't we get it over?"

"You little devil!" he said, and then: "For the last time, Susan, will you give me your word that when you're in London you'll only hack reasonable horses? This isn't the first time but about the *eighteenth* that I've asked you this! You keep buying these damned show young 'uns of yours that ought never to have left their damn grass country and start——"

"Trevor!" A very small voice indeed. "Trevor, nothing's ever happened, and it *does* do them good. I'm not quite a fool, you know, and I can do more with that sort of horse after three months in London than——"

"Will you be quiet! There's only one issue at present, and that is, will you or will you not promise me now that you'll stop it?"

"But, darling——"

"Will you or will you not give me your word now that you'll stop it?"

"I—Trevor—I wish you wouldn't look like that. I don't like it. I think it rather frightens me. *Please,* Trevor!"

"Will you or will you not give me your word?"

Again a silence, and then a smaller voice than any yet:

"Well, I s'pose I must." She stood up—a little and lovely figure. She said: "That's on one condition, dear, and a very important condition."

"Which is?" The man's voice had changed now. Once more she was close to him. Once more her hands were on his coat. She said:

"On the one condition—that you never look like that again. *Never!*"

His arms came out and closed round her. . . .

"And that," said Bird to Hewson, after coffee had been taken into the dining room one and three quarter hours later, "is that. All O. K. now. Look here, I'll catch him before he goes out. Anything you want to know?"

"Only what I told you. Farthing Flashlight."

Bird nodded; moved off with pontifical dignity. Inside the dining room talk had come back, pleasantly enough now, to Susan's adventure of the morning. Heath was saying:

"Wonder what sent her off like that? Some damn-fool kid, I suppose, with a handkerchief or something."

Susan shook her small head of smooth gold. "She's not that sort. Besides, I'd just passed about a dozen handkerchiefs and about a hundred and twenty motorcars all with their cutouts open, and she'd never taken what you could really call any notice at all. . . . No, it was very funny, Trevor. Just as we got opposite that opening facing what I call the Hyde Park Hotel gates—you know; just as we got there she seemed to jump about thirty feet forward, and then she was off. It was just as if somebody had hit her. Most extraordinary thing. . . . Trevor, what *is* the matter now?"

Heath had risen. Once more his face was set and pale. . . .

At a quarter to three there came a tap upon the door of Bird's pantry. Bird knew that tap. He did not worry himself to conceal the port. He called, and Hewson came in, a look of eager inquiry on his sharp face.

But Bird shook a great bald head. "Not our lucky day, m' lad."

Hewson sat down. "Damn it! Miss him or something? Or hasn't 'e gone yet?"

Bird drew down the corners of his mouth. "Oh, he's gone all right, blight him! And there *she* is, bless her, crying her eyes out in the libery! *I* don't know what's up to-day!"

Hewson scratched his head. "Thought you said they were all right at lunch?"

"And so they were. As all right as all right

may be. No, something else happened. Just after I'd taken in the coffee, they were all right then. Bit later, though, not more than five minutes, just as I was going by the dining room I could hear his voice: very angry, it was. I couldn't catch his words, but he was angry all right. I've never 'eard 'im like it, not even this morning. And then, just as I got past, the door flies open and out 'e comes. Doesn't wait for me nor nobody. Just grabs his hat and stick then, biff! the door's open, and bang! the door's shut. Exit Captain Trevor Heath and our chance of a few bob next week."

Hewson continued to scratch his head. "Fair knockout!" he said.

Bird nodded dolefully. "It is that! . . . Glass of port, son?"

"To tell you the truth," said Hewson, "I don't mind if I do. What's this? The 1901?"

" '08," said Bird. "It's better. You wait."

(3)

The room of Superintendent Pike was noiseless save for the heavy ticking of his clock and the busy scratching of his pen. He was finishing his final and confidential report on what the evening papers had been calling "The Great Contango Mystery." It was a good report, and he was pleased with it. He threw down his pen and with a sigh stretched and searched about in his pockets for pipe and tobacco.

His door opened to admit Jordan. Jordan was one of the Big Four and looked it. He was big enough, as people had often said, to be all of them.

"Finished?" he asked, and sat himself down upon a corner of Pike's table.

The table creaked. Pike nodded. He clipped together the seven buff sheets and handed them over.

"There it is, only don't read it in here. Study it by yourself to spare my blushes. It's all right, though."

Jordan folded the papers and slid them into his breast pocket. "Who's that," he said, "in your waiting room? Walking about like a tiger or something."

Pike started; pursed his lips into a silent whistle. "Gosh!" he said. "He's been waiting a bit longer than I meant." He reached out for a card that lay on the desk.

"Who is it?" said Jordan again. "I had a snoop at him through the transom. Face looks familiar somehow."

Pike read from the card. " 'Trevor Heath, The Uplands, Newmarket, Bucks Club' . . . Isn't that that . . ."

"That's it!" Jordan said. "Good bloke, I think. He's the lad that trained Whisky for the National last year, *and* rode him *and* won. Going to marry that Kerr girl, isn't he?"

Pike shrugged. "Not a racing man myself. You float off, and I'll see what he wants. Insisted on seeing *me,* for some reason."

Jordan went. Pike pressed a bell upon his desk. Within two minutes Trevor Heath was in the room. Pike rose to meet him. His long face was now gravely, lengthily official. After a murmured greeting he set a chair; sat down again himself. He said:

"I'm very sorry, sir. Afraid I've kept you waiting rather a long time. What can I do for you?"

From behind the official mask he studied his visitor. Sound man, he thought; straight, I'd say; angry or frightened. Or both. . . . Yes, probably both. . . .

Trevor Heath put hat and stick down upon the floor beside him. He sat upon the edge of his chair and leaned forward, staring at Pike. He said, without preamble:

"It's about my fiancée, Miss Susan Kerr. . . ."

Pike repressed a start. He remembered the name now, Susan Kerr . . . Susan Kerr . . . He knew her—one of those people who had been in that house at Polferry; that very odd house party at Polferry; that house party at Polferry which Pike, for Scotland Yard's sake and his own, would rather forget. He said, with a polite resignation he was far from feeling:

"Miss Kerr, sir? Is that the daughter of Sir David and Lady Kerr?"

Heath nodded. "Yes. And I think you know it, Superintendent. They wanted me outside to see somebody else, but I wouldn't see anybody else because I happen to know—I know from Susan, as a matter of fact—that you're the man who went down to Polferry from the Yard about the murder of Mrs. Hale-Storford. That's right, isn't it?"

Pike nodded. It was a cautious movement but definite assent.

"Right! . . . Forgive me—I can't tell you this sitting down. I must get up and walk about." He jerked himself out of his chair and began to stride about the room. Pike sat still, following him with his eyes.

"Don't quite know where to begin," Heath was saying. He spoke savagely. Pike's gaze noted his pallor, his jerkiness; saw that some great force was moving the man. Pike said gently:

"Try the beginning, sir. From what you say I gather it's got some connection with the Polferry murder."

"Some connection! By God, it has!" Heath was at the table now. He stood leaning his hands upon it, gazing down at Pike with eyes that seemed afire. He said:

"All right, I'll try it. You know that Polferry case. You know—whether you say so officially or not—you know yourself that the Hale-Storford woman was killed by someone in that house. Don't you?"

Pike's long face did not change its expression. He said quietly:

"Answered your own question, haven't you, sir? Please go on. Wouldn't it be better if you sat down?"

"Sat down!" said Heath. "Sat down! That's what everybody's been doing, especially you people up here. Just sitting doing nothing, while there's some damn fiend about who's killing—yes, man, *killing* I said—and after he's killed, just laughing at you up his foul sleeve."

"Try sitting down, sir." Pike's woodenness seemed, paradoxically, to have a soothing effect. Heath sat down. He was silent a moment, fighting obviously for self-control. He said at last:

"Sorry! Been making a bit of a fool of myself. But this thing's beginning to shake me up. . . . Look here, Superintendent, has it ever occurred to you to wonder at all about those other two deaths?"

Pike's expression was a mild question. Heath jerked himself about in his chair. He said:

"Yes, yes! I suppose you can't answer leading questions like that. I won't ask any more. I'll say this, though. It *has* occurred to me to wonder about them. First the Hale-Storford woman, and though it's murder nobody can find out who did it. Then her sister, and that *looks* like an accident. And then that kid Anstruther, and *that* looks like an accident too."

"One moment, sir!" Pike had weighed up his man. He had decided apparently to become human. He said:

"You must realize, sir, that whatever the papers and the writers of detective stories say, we're not all fools up here. I admit that the Hale-Storford death got us guessing, but then as you might say, there must be cases every now and then which would get the Archangel Gabriel guessing. In regard to these two subsequent deaths, sir—well, not being fools, as I've said, and the coincidence being what it was, we naturally looked into those very, very carefully.

A lot more carefully than they would have been looked into, I might tell you, in the ordinary course. And the result was——"

"Yes?" said Heath eagerly, leaning forward until he almost slipped off his chair.

"The result, sir, was that we found there was no occasion whatsoever for supposing that the deaths were due to anything but bona fide accidents. In the second case it was found that the plug in the boat which Mr. Anstruther was sailing was faulty—and that happens to many boats at many times; in the first case—well, I don't know whether you know Polferry Hill, sir, but it's a very dangerous road indeed for anyone, let alone a lady, to drive down at night. As a matter of fact, the Council have been considering doing something to make it safer for the last two years. Unfortunately they've only been considering. It's only a twenty-six-foot road, and along parts of it there's practically a sheer drop on the off side. It was at one of those points that Miss Rossiter swerved and tipped over. What led her to swerve it's impossible to tell, but it's also impossible to say that such a thing couldn't be an accident. In fact, such accidents happen practically all day, as you might say, and every day. . . . Now, sir, you go on."

Heath seemed more at ease now. He sat back in his chair and crossed one long horseman's leg over the other. He even looked at Pike with the beginnings of a smile. He said:

"I say, you know, you're being very decent to me, aren't you? . . . Right, I'll go on. What would you say, Superintendent, if I were to tell you that unless somebody does something and does something quickly and thoroughly there's going to be *another* accident?"

Pike pursed his lips. It was the only movement in the long face, but his small brown eyes were very keen. He said, after a pause:

"P'r'aps you'd go on, sir. You haven't told me much yet, you know. When you've given me your grounds for saying what you said just now, then perhaps I'll tell you what my views would be."

Heath, now that he had been drawing near to his real point, became restless again. He grunted apology; got up from his chair; once more began to pace about the room. Pike sat solid, only his eyes moving as they followed the figure of his visitor.

"The accident," said Heath, in a tone so savage that momentarily Pike almost lost his mask of composure, "the *accident, if* someone doesn't do something, is going to be to Miss Kerr. This morning, while Miss Kerr was riding in the Row, somebody did something to her horse which made it bolt. Miss Kerr might easily have been killed.

"About three weeks ago, when Miss Kerr was driving back at night from Ranelagh, a big car, going very fast indeed, came straight at her as she turned into the main road out of Ferrier's Lane. Miss Kerr was alone in the car. Because she's a very fine driver indeed, and because she's got the nerve of about ten men, she got away with her life. Instead of braking, as ninety-nine out of a hundred women would have done, she slammed her foot down on the accelerator. As it was, this car smashed into the rear of hers and actually took off her spare wheel. She stopped her car and hopped out, but she wasn't quick enough. The other one had gone. She couldn't read the number; there was no rearlight. That's *One!*"

Heath fell silent for a moment. He walked round until once more he was standing by his chair. Pike saw that his pallor had increased. He said, leaning his hands upon Pike's table:

"That's One! Now Two: Ten days ago Miss Kerr and I were coming out of the Diplomat's Theatre, again at night. You know the sort of scrum there is there as a rule. It's a very small place, and the exits are very wide, and the crowd simply surges out. I left Miss Kerr on the curb while I went for a taxi. I was very lucky, I got one quick. I perched on the step and came back with him—coming down, that is, from the corner of Shaftesbury Avenue. I suppose we were about twenty-five yards from her—I could see her quite plainly—when there seemed to be a sudden lurch forward of the mob behind her. . . ."

Pike, who had been listening intently, but with his eyes fixed upon his blotter, looked up in surprise at the sudden silence. Heath had covered his eyes with his hand, but almost immediately he straightened himself, dropped the hand, and went on. But now his voice was the level flat voice of the man who is determined at all costs to be unemotional. He said:

"We were, as I say, about twenty-five yards away when I saw this sudden surge of the crowd. There was a bus coming up the road, coming up, that is, on the same side as the theatre. This what I have called lurch of the crowd seemed to shoot Miss Kerr forward. She fell sprawling into the road right in front of the bus. Again through good driving—this time the bus driver's—Miss Kerr was saved. How that man stopped the bus as he did I don't know. He had to skid her to do it. When it was finished Miss Kerr's head was lying about two inches off his near-hind wheel. She wasn't hurt at all. By the time I'd got up and seen her all right and thanked the bus driver and answered the damn fool questions some officious bobby was asking, it was too late to *do* anything. I didn't say anything to the bobby, but I went about among the people who'd stayed to look. All they could tell me was that somebody coming down the steps of the theatre behind the press on the pavement had seemed to stumble. A man, they thought it was, but even that they weren't sure of. Anyhow, they said that this stumble seemed to push everybody forward on top of everybody else, and Miss Kerr was the last one, and not being ready—well, I've told you what happened. . . . That's two, Superintendent, *two*. Two of your *accidents* in under three weeks. But that wasn't enough. To-day we got Number Three. I've told you about that."

He seemed about to say more; then closed his mouth. He sat down. He waited.

Pike raised his eyes from the picture he had been drawing on his blotting pad. His voice was devoid of expression; now even his eyes seemed guarded. He said:

"Yes, sir. This third one you talk about—the horse accident, I take it you mean—can you tell me anything more about that?"

Heath hitched up his chair. He rested an elbow upon the table and his chin upon his hand. He seemed suddenly tired. He said:

"I can. This afternoon, with the groom, I examined that horse. The groom showed me something that he had found, not at once when he brought the horse home, but later, when he was dressing him. What he had found was a little, very deep puncture in the near quarter. When he first found it, it'd had a drop of blood congealed on the top. When he removed this scab fresh blood had welled up at once. Even when *I* saw the horse, less than two hours ago, fresh blood would well up each time the scab was taken away."

"I know nothing of horses, sir," said Pike's quiet voice. "Have you ever seen a small wound of this description before on a horse?"

Heath shrugged; an impatient movement. He said:

"How the devil can I tell you? It's the sort of place which might be made by any sharp thing which had been jabbed into the horse. I may have seen a hundred. If I had, I should never've remembered them enough to have noticed 'em. . . . Tell you what, this was about the kind of place a horsefly would make, but multiplied by about twenty."

"And it couldn't have been a horsefly, sir?"

"My dear feller! . . ."

"I see, sir. And it's impossible to account for this mark on the horse in any ordinary way. It couldn't have got it in the stable?"

"Absolutely impossible."

"And you think that whatever caused this mark . . ."

"Made the horse bolt? Yes, I do. I don't think, I *know!* What Miss Kerr told me of the way the horse started off is proof."

"Are you trying to tell me, sir"—Pike's voice was still a level, official monotone—"that you think this wound was caused by someone deliberately, with the intention of making the horse bolt?"

"Damn it, man! That's what I'm saying, isn't it?"

"All right, sir. Don't let's get heated. I'm only trying to get to the bottom of this. Now, if you think that, will you also tell me how you think the wound was caused?"

Heath shook his head wearily. "You've got me there. Can't have been done by anyone else mounted, because Miss Kerr knows there was no one near her. Anyhow, you can't very well lean over and jab a spike into another feller's horse without being spotted. And I don't see how it could possibly have been caused by anyone on foot. You can't get near enough to the other side of the railings, for one thing, and anyhow, Miss Kerr says she was quite twelve feet from the edge of the tan."

For a moment Pike's eyes looked straight into his visitor's. Pike said very slowly:

"So you have no idea at all, sir, how this could have been done? . . . No idea at all?"

Heath laughed. A surprising sound, but it was a laugh which had no mirth in it. He said:

"Well, I've got a damn-fool idea, but it's not the sort of idea you could say in cold blood at Scotland Yard."

Again Pike looked at him. *"Is* your blood cold, sir?" he said.

Heath stared for a moment. Then: "By God, it's not!" he said. "You're right. Well, I'll tell you: laugh if you like. I think that place on that horse was made by a large-sized slug from a large-sized air pistol."

"And that that air pistol," Pike broke in, "was fired from a motorcar, either stationary or moving slowly along that side of the road nearest to Miss Kerr?"

Again Heath stared. "By God! That's exactly what I do think!" he said. "You don't mean to tell me you agree?"

Pike shrugged. "Can't go as far as that, sir, but certainly the idea had occurred to me while you were talking."

Heath leaned forward in his chair and took out a cigarette case from his hip pocket. "Have a smoke," he said, and held out the case. Suddenly Pike sloughed officialdom completely. His lantern face cracked into one of his disarming grins. He said:

"Very kind of you, sir. I will."

There was silence while two cigarettes were lighted, and while, in part, at least, they were smoked. It was Heath who spoke first. He flicked ash into Pike's ash tray and said:

"Well? What are you going to do?"

Pike looked at him. "I'll be frank with you, sir. I don't know. After what you've told me I've got to talk the matter over with my superiors." He looked at his watch. It was four o'clock. "If you'll give me a telephone number, sir, I'll ring you up at, let me see, half-past five. Will that do?"

Heath got to his feet. He bent down and picked up hat and stick. He said, straightening himself:

"Thank you. It will."

He held out his hand; he smiled. "You must forgive my madness," he said. "But this isn't exactly . . ."

Pike shook the hand. "I quite see, sir, and if I may say so, I sympathize. Very difficult position."

(4)

Heath, now in a dinner jacket, for it was seven o'clock and more, sat where he had sat in the afternoon. Across the table he stared at Pike, in his blue eyes a sort of baffled, hopeless anger which knows itself unreasonable. He was saying:

"That's final, is it?"

Pike nodded gravely. "I'm sorry, sir, it is. After all, Captain Heath, you must, as a man of intelligence, see the chief's point of view. In spite of the very flimsy evidence—now, don't fly at me, sir, because, if you look at it from our point of view, flimsy it is—in spite of that, the chief said that he would be prepared to give Miss Kerr police protection for a reasonable period *if* she herself were to apply for it. You say that you've tried Miss Kerr and that Miss Kerr won't hear of such a thing."

Miserably Heath nodded. "That's right. I didn't tell you before, but we've had God Almighty's own row about it."

Pike shrugged. "Exactly, sir. Well, what can we do? Miss Kerr won't apply; she's the party concerned . . ." His voice trailed off into silence.

Heath got up. "Well, I suppose there's nothing for it. I shall have to knock off work and do the job myself."

"Look here, sir." Pike rose with his visitor. He was entirely human now; nothing about

him of the policeman. "Look here, sir," he said
again, "if you take my advice you'll patch up
that quarrel with Miss Kerr. I hope you don't
think I'm being impertinent, sir, but I've a reason for it. Patch it up, and then you can keep
next to her. And if you see anything which
seems to you corroborative of what you've seen
to-day, you get onto the nearest telephone and
let me know. And then—well, I can't promise
—but *I'll* do my level best to help you."

Heath endeavoured to smile, failing rather
wretchedly. "Right-ho, I'll do that. You've been
very decent to me, you know, Superintendent.
. . . I say! Is it any good, any good at all, my
getting her people to—— Oh, damn! They're
away, but I expect I could cable 'em."

Pike considered. "Miss Kerr—is she a minor,
sir?"

"Good Lord, no! She's twenty-five."

Pike shook his head gloomily. "Sorry, sir,
afraid that wouldn't be much good. The chief
was very definite."

"All right." Heath's tone was blackly de-
spondent. He picked up his hat. "I must do the

whole blasted job myself. I suppose you're right and we must patch up the quarrel. But of all the blasted silly ways——" He cut himself short. He snapped open the hat and turned round, holding out his hand. "Good-night, Superintendent I won't forget what you've told me. As soon as I hear anything, you bet I'll telephone you."

Pike shook the hand and opened the door. But as soon as he had opened it he shut it again. He said:

"Half a minute, sir. Half a minute!" He seemed excited. He also seemed as if he were trying to make up his mind. Apparently he made it up for he said:

"Look here, sir. If I give you a bit of advice, a sort of tip, *as a purely private person,* will you take it as coming from a purely private person? Even keep my name out of it?"

Heath looked at him and nodded. A nod which Pike found, looking at him, as decisive and satisfactory as many a man's oath. Pike said, dropping his voice:

"It's this, sir. D'you happen to know by any chance Colonel Gethryn?"

"Gethryn?" Heath's voice showed rather incredulous surprise. "Yes, I know him, but where did you get the 'Colonel' from?"

Pike smiled. "I know he don't like having the rank used, sir."

"But he isn't a colonel, man! Lord, Sam Gethryn hasn't even got enough brains to ride a horse properly, although he does try."

Pike shook his head. "Oh, no, sir, no! I think you must be meaning some other gentleman of the same name. Colonel Anthony Gethryn, I mean, sir. You must have heard——"

"Oh, that one!" Heath's tone too showed signs of excitement. "And now I come to think of it he's some sort of cousin of Sam's. Why?"

"Well, if you could get hold of him in some way or other and put your trouble to him, I believe you might do yourself and me—everybody, in fact—a good turn. I wanted Colonel Gethryn to come in on this Hale-Storford case right from the beginning, but he couldn't at the time. Knowing him as I do, I should think he'd been away quite long enough, even for him. If you could get him, sir . . . what I mean, if he *did* take an interest in this, I think something might begin to happen. I can't ask him myself, even unofficially."

"I see." Again Heath held out his hand. Again they shook. "You're a good fellow, you know. Wait and see whether you hear anything from me."

The door closed behind him. Pike crossed over to his table, sat upon it, and began to fill a pipe. A slow grin wreathed its way across his face. He began to whistle to himself, two semitones flat: "Won't you come home, Bill Bailey?"

CHAPTER FIVE

AT HALF-PAST seven in the evening of June sixteenth—two days, that is, after Trevor Heath's
interview with Pike—these two men met again.
They did not know until meet they did that
meet they were going to. All, in fact, that each
knew until that time, was that he was to dine
with and at the house of a suddenly returned
Anthony Gethryn.

Pike was early; Heath, late. Pike and Anthony were, indeed having their second glass of
sherry when Heath arrived. He shook hands
with his host, but even while he was shaking
hands he was staring not at his host but at his
fellow guest.

"Exactly!" Anthony surveyed them with
something of benevolence in his look. "Exactly.
I said a small party, and a small party it is. You
can see it all. All boys together. I'd like to suggest that for the first part of dinner, at any rate,

we talk fluff. When I say, 'Go!' then we will go. Agreed?"

That first part of dinner became—so good was the dinner, so, at least provocative of good talk the wine—the whole of dinner. It was not until White had left the room and the port was upon the table that business began. Then it was Anthony who started it. He said:

"You know, Heath, you ought to congratulate yourself. On being, I mean, the most persuasive letter writer in my experience."

Heath smiled a smile that was rather awry. "I've got something," he said, "to be persuasive about. In fact, I'm not sure I oughtn't to be somewhere near it now instead of here, but still . . ."

Pike filled his glass from the decanter and pushed the decanter farther on its travel. He said, looking at Heath:

"By the way, sir, I suppose nothing else has turned up?"

Heath shook his head. "No, damn it! D'you know, I suppose I ought to be glad, but I'm sorry."

"Nothing at all?" said Pike.

"Absolutely nothing at all."

"This," said Anthony, "is cryptic. I suppose I'm right in inferring that this something is a further *accident* involving or nearly involving Miss Susan Kerr?"

Heath nodded. And Pike said:

"That's quite right, sir." He looked at Anthony with his long face held rather on one side. He added:

"And if I might, sir, I should like to take a small bet with you."

"It is, Pike?"

"It is, sir, that even before Captain Heath's letter to you, you'd thought of putting a finger into this pie."

Anthony grinned. "Bet's off, Pike. You've won." His grin faded as quickly as it had come. "Only *thought* though, mind you. You see, until you wrote to me, Heath, I hadn't got, really, a decent excuse for butting in. But now I have. Look here! I'll tell you what I'd like to do. I'd like to give you my idea—made up from what I've heard, what I've read in the papers and what you've told me in your letter—of the situation as it affects you and everyone to-day. Where I'm wrong, you fellows can put me right. That suit?"

Heath nodded.

"I should say so," said Pike.

"Right. On the sixteenth September Mrs. Hale-Storford died as the result of a wound in the throat. On the twentieth of November, Miss Miriam Rossiter, Mrs. Hale-Storford's sister, died as the result of a motor accident. On April thirtieth, George Anstruther was drowned as the result of a boating accident. On the twentieth of May Miss Susan Kerr has a narrow escape from almost certain death in a motoring accident. On the first of June she has a narrow escape from being run over by an omnibus. On the tenth of June, six days ago, she has a narrow escape from death or serious injury by reason of her horse bolting. Your contention, Heath, is that these three misadventures were not chance misadventures; were, in other words, not accidents at all, but the results of deliberate intentions on the part of some person or persons. You go farther than this, I think, and say that the cause of these misadventures is or are the same person or persons who caused the death of George Anstruther and Miriam Rossiter.

"You've endeavoured to persuade Miss Kerr of what you consider her danger but have failed entirely. Because you've failed, it's impossible for you to obtain protection for Miss Kerr. You want, therefore, something done to prove, first, that the *accidents* causing the deaths of Miriam Rossiter and George Anstruther were not, in fact, accidents at all but murders; consequently and secondly, you want the person or persons responsible for these murders caught before they can carry out any fresh schemes in regard to Miss Kerr. . . . How many marks do I get for that?"

"So far as I'm concerned," said Heath, "a hundred per cent."

Pike nodded agreement.

"My next move, then," Anthony began.

But he was interrupted. Heath cut him short. "I say—I say!" said Heath, "just a minute! Not a hundred after all. Didn't you say just now, that I thought that whoever it was who'd been trying these tricks on Susan was the same person who'd tried 'em successfully on Anstruther and the Rossiter woman?"

"I did."

"Well, didn't you leave something out, if that was all you said?"

Anthony shook his head. "Don't think so. How?"

Heath, seeming to labour under some great excitement, flung out an arm. He knocked over his glass, and the port made a dark stain upon the white cloth. He did not notice it. He pointed a finger at Anthony. He said in a voice which sounded hoarse:

"What about the first death? What about the Hale-Storford woman herself?"

"My dear chap," said Anthony. "What do you say to that, Pike?"

Pike shook his head. Pike was not committing himself. Pike said with a half smile:

"You go on, sir. This is your party."

"But my dear feller," Heath began.

Anthony pushed the decanter toward him.

"You pick up that glass and fill it. Also, give me a chance. You think that the killer of Eve Hale-Storford is going on with his killing. I don't. Look what you're saying. You're saying, in effect, that the killer of Eve Hale-Storford was either Hale-Storford himself, or Dorothy Graye, his housekeeper, or Banner (R.N. retired) or Trenchard (God knows what!). You *are* saying that. You must be saying that, because, of the other four people who were in the house on the night of Eve Hale-Storford's death, that woman herself, Miriam Rossiter, and George Anstruther are dead, and Miss Kerr (I am speaking all the time from this point of view of yours) has been the subject of attempts at her death. Now examine the four you have left. You are saying, in effect, that either Dorothy Graye alone; or the triumvirate of men without Dorothy Graye; or the whole quartette composed of that triumvirate *and* Dorothy Graye are your murderers. I submit that that theory is pure. . . . I should say that that theory won't hold water. Or not enough water, at any rate. Look at it!

"I can't believe that Hale-Storford, a noted doctor; Banner, a retired naval man of the usual respectability of naval men; and Trenchard could together be this murder club or even part of it. This sort of crime is not committed by such a chance assortment of hitherto ordinarily peaceable men. I don't know, but I'm going to chance the guess that Pike, when we ask him, will tell us that at least two of this trio had never met before the night of Eve Hale-Storford's death; that all their pasts have been rigorously examined and are as blameless as may be; that there is no apparently possible or probable link which would bind them into a sort of Sudden Death Unlimited Combine. . . . Go on, Pike, blast me out of the water, if you can."

Pike beamed benevolence over his glass. His eyes, although the smile had touched them, were bright and very shrewd. He said:

"You know I can't, sir. You're quite right. That three have been under the microscope, so to say. And it's no mere probability that they weren't together, sir; it's as near a cast-iron certainty as you'll get in a month of leap years."

Anthony raised his glass and drank. "Thank you, Pike. . . . Now, Heath, it's no more likely that any one of those three men is by himself the author of these three deaths than that they all were. For if one of them was the original murderer of Eve Hale-Storford, he must have been such murderer with the knowledge of the other two, or they wouldn't have backed up his alibi by swearing that on the night that Eve Hale-Storford was killed he didn't leave the room between the time when the upstairs party went to bed and the time when they themselves went upstairs and discovered her body. . . . Follow me, Heath?"

Heath nodded slowly. "Go on, will you?" he said. There was a frown of concentration between his brows; he was chewing a cigar as yet unlighted.

Pike, looking at him covertly from the other side of the table, was shocked to see the change which only four days had wrought in the man. The thin face was yet thinner. It was now, indeed, almost gaunt and the blue eyes had black rings of sleeplessness beneath them.

Anthony went on. Anthony said:

"Right. We've done away with Hale-Storford plus Banner plus Trenchard, and we've done away with Hale-Storford *or* Banner *or* Trenchard. We have left Dorothy Graye, and that —yes, I can see you grinning, Pike—is absurd. I'm going to have another guess. I'm going to chance my arm—a bit more risky this time—I bet you ten to one that Pike, when I ask him, will tell us truthfully that Dorothy Graye hasn't left the Watch House. That Dorothy Graye couldn't have been the author of the two successful *accidents* nor the author of the three unsuccessful attempts on Miss Kerr. . . . Look at him, Heath, and you'll see that I'm right without waiting for him to speak. . . . So, Heath, we're without Dorothy Graye as well. Now what?"

Heath put his head in his hands. He ran his fingers through his sleek fair hair until it stood up in little tufts. He said from under those hands:

"I'm with you, of course. Very clear and perfectly logical and all that. But what's it come to? Nonsense. Nonsense or magic! And I don't believe in either of those, Gethryn. Don't know about you." His blue eyes blazed suddenly. He raised a hand and turned it into a fist and thumped the table with it until the glasses rang. "For God's sake, man, let's have some sense, not theorizing—however clever it is!"

"Easy, man, easy!" Anthony's tone was as compelling as it was sympathetic. "Don't take it so hard. And don't let your troubles run away with your reasoning. Perhaps I've been annoying. I'm always being told I am. But I think you've missed something. All I was doing was to show you, in effect, that in all probability—in so much probability that we must, at least at this stage, take it as certainty—the murderer of Eve Hale-Storford did *not* cause the *accidents.*"

Once more Heath put his head in his hands. The other two men were silent. When he raised his head it was to show them a face so ravaged with a miserable hopelessness that both the watchers, despite their utter innocence, felt immediately a sense of personal guilt. At this face Anthony stared a moment. He said contritely:

"My dear fellow! You've got me wrong again. I see now that you think I am trying to say that your accidents aren't real ones. In other words, that you're wrong about them. I'm not saying that I believe you about those accidents. I'd begun to believe you before I knew of your existence. Now, listen to this and grip onto it. All I told you, boiled down, comes to this: *that the murderer of Eve Hale-Storford was not the author of the accidents.* That, in other words, one person or set of persons killed Eve Hale-Storford, and another person or set of persons has killed Anstruther and the woman Rossiter and is trying to kill Miss Kerr. Get that?"

The relief that Heath felt was shown by his first broad smile of the evening.

"I always was a bally fool," he said. "Yes, I've got you now. Go on, will you? I don't understand where you're getting to, but I do understand up to now. Go on, will you?"

Anthony smiled. "Now, we can assume, first,

that the murderer of Eve Hale-Storford was someone within the house. Secondly, we can assume that the author of the accidents is some other person (in each case I am using the singular number for convenience) within the house; in each case, again, I am using the expression 'within the house' to mean someone who was in the Watch House on the night of Eve Hale-Storford's death. Now, to take a primary view of this business—and let me tell you that the primary view is often the sanest and best— which person within the house would you say was the most injured by the act of the original murder?"

"Husband," said Heath.

"Exactly. Hale-Storford. I think Pike will tell you, as indeed he may have already, that Hale-Storford had the reputation of being utterly devoted to his wife; that he was as nearly knocked over by her death as a man can be. Will you, Pike?"

"I will, sir." Pike was emphatic. "I should say beyond all possibility of play-acting."

Anthony nodded. "Right. Hale-Storford is

the most genuinely injured person and also therefore a genuinely innocent person. Therefore, again, both Banner and Trenchard are innocent persons. Witness my previous remarks this evening. Therefore, and here once again we come back to the primary view, the guilty person was one of the upstairs party which was composed, besides the murdered woman herself, of Susan Kerr, Miriam Rossiter, Dorothy Graye, and George Anstruther. Now, Heath, Miss Kerr belonged to that upstairs party. Accidents, unsuccessful so far, have happened to her. Miriam Rossiter belonged to that upstairs party, but a successful accident happened to her. George Anstruther belonged to that upstairs party, and a successful accident happened to him.

"If, before we break up *this* party to-night, we ask Pike, officially or unofficially, to find out for us exactly where Hale-Storford was and what he was doing on the days when these unsuccessful accidents happened to Miss Kerr, what shall we have?"

Once more Heath struck the table with his fist, but this time not in despair. He said:

"Good God! I've got you." He looked with eagerness almost dreadful at Pike. "Have you? Do *you* see what he's at?"

Pike nodded. "I've worked with Colonel Gethryn before, and if I hadn't, I think I should."

The words were barely out of his mouth before Heath was talking again. Heath was saying, almost shouting: "But, look here, man, why don't you ask him this too?—why don't you ask him what Hale-Storford was doing at the times of the two successful *accidents.*"

Anthony smiled. "Easy, easy, Heath. I shan't ask him that because, knowing the man, I bet he's done it already and, knowing him, I bet he'd have told us already if there was something there to get hold of. Is that so, Pike?"

"It is, sir. Very much so."

"I see," said Heath. "I see. But, look here, Gethryn, what can you do even if Pike *can* tell us that Hale-Storford was in the neighbourhood of Susan's accidents every time she had them? Hale-Storford can't be a fool—in fact, by God! he must be as clever as Satan—and just the mere fact of his being near doesn't give you anything you can catch hold of him with, does it? . . . And if you can't catch hold of him you're still . . . My God! all I want out of this job's to make sure that Susan's safe. Feller must be mad—mad!"

"Of course he is, my dear fellow! Mad as a March hare!" Anthony's tone in its everyday-ness was soothing.

"Good Losh, sir!" Pike burst out, "I think I must have been wandering or something. I've only just got to the full meaning of what you're giving us. D'you mean to say that this young doctor, this decent man that was so knocked over when his wife was dead, that he's been so knocked off his balance by not knowing how his wife died that he's—that he's—that he's——" Pike felt at a loss for words.

"Exactly what I do mean. It's the one ex-planation, the one reasonable explanation. There's a fellow, brilliant, possibly—who can tell?—a little unbalanced always, probably by

reason of that very brilliancy aided by over-
work. He falls in love, desperately in love. He
gets married, he's happy, he's married for six
months, and then, snap!—just like that, his
wife's killed. And he *knows*—as all the world
knows, Pike, but as all the world can do nothing
about—he *knows* that someone in that house—
that someone of that upstairs lot I've been talking about—did it. The Law fumbles about (I'm
putting this from his point of view, mind you)—
the Law fumbles about and gets nowhere. By
letting the four *who must contain the killer* go
free, the Law refuses him even the satisfaction
of civilized revenge. So, being a man who can
think for himself—and he does, in fact, think
too much for himself—he decided to exact pun-
ishment himself. As I see it, he probably works
like this: He thinks and thinks. He thinks round
the subject and round it. Brooding, half insane,
and half coldly calculating, he makes up his
mind. He says to himself: *'That's the one!'* and
he points the finger in his mind at his wife's sister. And so, somehow, he brings about the death,

in such a way that it won't incriminate himself at all, of that sister.

"But where is he after the first thrill of having carried out this execution has died away? Nowhere. Or, rather, he's back where he started from. He finds that what he had held in his turgid, unresting mind as a certainty now seems only the wildest of guesses, and like all guesses, possibly wrong. He looks round. There are still three left. He begins all over again. Soon he has persuaded himself that his first execution was wrong. That, in the state he is in, is no matter. What he must do is to make another execution; this time the right one. He thinks round and about the remaining three. He chooses, at last, the boy Anstruther, and so the boy Anstruther dies too. And then, very soon, the whole vicious circle again. Once more that finger in his brain points round, settles on. . . Well, you see what I'm driving at." Anthony cut himself short here. He looked sidelong and a little anxiously at Heath.

Heath, his elbows upon the table, his chin upon his fist, was staring into nothingness. He said in a toneless voice which yet was more expressive of feeling than any cry:

"My God, man! That's awful! Awful! And we must sit here in this room all comfortable and warm and talk about it. Just talk, talk, talk!" His voice began to rise. "Why don't we stop talking? Why don't we *do* something? Why don't we get hold of this mad devil and kill him or put him somewhere where he can't . . ."

His voice died away. Anthony was anxious and looked it. He said earnestly:

"My dear fellow, you mustn't pay much attention to me. I know I've been talking a lot, but, after all, I've only been talking conjecture. I'm afraid I've been a bit too——"

Heath cut in. "You haven't been too anything! You're right, you're right. Any fool could see that you're right."

He suddenly straightened in his chair. He shot out an arm. The rigid fingers, quivering, pointed at Pike. "Tell him, tell him and his lot it's up to them. They're the people we pay to look after us. Isn't it up to them? . . ."

Anthony got out of his chair, came round the

table, and laid a hand upon the quivering shoulder. "Easy, man, easy! You can't accept impossibilities. Suppose the police were to listen to every silly, self-satisfied ass like myself, where should we be then? None of us'd be safe."

Pike rose too. He said, leaning his hands upon the table and looking straight at Heath:

"Look here, sir, don't you worry too much. It's me, you remember, who put you on to getting Colonel Gethryn to come home. And I'm as thankful as you are that come home he has. Just at the moment what Colonel Gethryn says about the police not being able to do anything is right. But it's only right just for the moment. Because I know Colonel Gethryn, sir, and I know myself. And with those two bits of knowledge put together I know this: that, having got where we are in what Colonel Gethryn calls 'pure conjecture' but which I call something else a good deal better, we'll very soon get on to a point when we *can* do what we want—act. It's quite true that officially I can't do anything, yet, but it's also true that neither Colonel Gethryn nor I am going to just leave things at pure talk. We're going to get on with it. You bear that in mind, sir. We'll all play our cards properly, and no harm will come to your lady."

With a hand which showed its shaking by the rattling of the decanter against his glass, Heath poured himself wine. He drank it at a gulp. He straightened himself in his chair. He said, looking round:

"I'm sorry, you fellows! Seem to be always making a fool of myself nowadays. What's to do, then? You two talk, I'll shut up."

Over Heath's head Anthony looked at Pike. He said:

"Mean to tell me, Pike, that you've swallowed my stuff too?"

"Lock, sir, stock, and barrel," said Pike. "I wonder why the blink I didn't see it before."

Suddenly Anthony grinned. Something of his usual self returned to him. He said:

"If you go on like this I'll begin to believe it myself. . . . Well, Pike, Heath said it. What's to do?"

"Ask me that, sir, and I'll ask you. I'm official; you're not. What are *you* going to do? Captain Heath's got *his* job."

"I," said Anthony, "am going to ring the bell, thus, and when White comes in, as he does, within forty-five seconds—thus—I'm going to say to him, 'White, in the morning just see that the car's ready for a long trip. Pack enough stuff for me for three days and yourself. If you've got any spare time after that you can spend it with a map, looking out the best route to Polferry on the Wessex coast.'"

Behind White the door clicked softly. Anthony said:

"The party will now adjourn to another department. We will now entirely bar shop. The best thing, I think, that we can do for the next hour is to settle down to some really serious eighteenth-century drinking."

CHAPTER SIX

Trewarth Arms Hotel,
Morlock,
Wessex.

17th June, 193–.

DEAR HEATH:

Important. Please get Miss Kerr—or do it your-self—to put in all the Social Columns a statement to the effect that she is leaving for Scotland to-morrow. Then let her stay in London, you sticking by her as close as usual, if not closer.

Explanations later.

Yours sincerely,
A. R. GETHRYN.

(2)

Trewarth Arms Hotel,
Morlock,
Wessex.

17th June, 193–.

DEAR PIKE:

Something for you. As you see, I am staying some way from Polferry, but I was over there all the morning. So was White. I had no luck, but White did. He got hold of the boatman who had sold the yawl *Bluebird* to Hale-Storford. There is the permanent bad time on for boatmen, and old Tresillian had no objection to drinking beer so long as White went on paying for it. White, on instructions and enough money, did go on paying for it. He did not, being a man of some experience, start upon his real subject until the old man was on his seventh pint. But when he did start, he seems to have worked fast. Result: Tresillian grew boozily critical of 'the doctor's' care, before 'the young gentleman' met his death, of the *Bluebird*. Hale-Storford, as you are sure to know, bought the *Bluebird* about a month after his wife's death; *but*—and here's something you don't know because it never came out at the Anstruther inquest, and until he met White the old man never breathed the words—Tresillian was, for about ten days preceding Anstruther's fatal trip, telling Hale-Storford that the seams of *Bluebird* wanted repitching and the plug replacing. At the inquest, you will remember, Hale-Storford said that he had put in a new plug; that he supposed that it was something to do with this plug's newness which caused it to be driven out and so let the boat fill. That plug, you will also remember, was never found. Now, Tresillian told White this morning that he didn't believe this plug story; that he was sure no new plug had ever, in fact, been put in. The old man, mind you, wasn't suggesting or even trying to suggest that there was anything deliberate about Hale-Storford's omission, but he holds that 'the doctor' had never replaced the old plug.

I know there's nothing in all this which the official mind (all right! I'm not getting at you personally) will be able to allow itself to take hold of enough to warrant any action. I give it to you as just one further stick to place upon the pile of confirmation.

You'll hear from me again to-morrow. I'm going to be busy this afternoon. Have you sounded Lucas about this matter? If so, give him this letter to read at once. If not, pass it on to him after you've told him the tale.

Yours,

A. R. G.

(3)

(Telegram handed in at Morlock at 1 P. M. 18th June, 193–. Received Kensington Gore at 2:5 P. M.)

LUCAS 112 VERE MANSIONS S W
        HAVE YOU SEEN PIKE STOP IF NOT DO SO STOP BOTH COME DOWN HERE TOMORROW MIDDAY EXPRESS STOP FISHING SUCCESSFUL STOP GARDEN LOVELY
GETHRYN

(4)

"Which shows," said Lucas, "just what we do think of you."

Anthony grinned. "I know. A damn nuisance, but better take some notice of him."

"That is," Lucas agreed, "roughly what I mean. And now, perhaps, after wasting this hour—well, perhaps not wasting, it was a good meal—perhaps you will tell us exactly why we're here. Eh, Pike?"

Pike shrugged. Pike permitted himself a joke. Pike said:

"Perhaps he will, sir, perhaps he won't. Either way, nothing we can say will alter it."

"You are here," said Anthony, "to be persuaded. To be persuaded that you have grounds for, if not the immediate arrest, at least the watching of Hale-Storford while you rake up a case against him."

"Are we indeed?" said Lucas. He strove to keep his tone calm and tolerantly disbelieving. He did not notably succeed; too much of his real interest, almost excitement, showed through.

Pike did not attempt to dissemble; he leaned across the table. He said eagerly:

"Where is he, sir?"

Anthony smiled, shaking his head. "I don't know, Pike. If I were to make a guess, I should say somewhere between St. Pancras and Carlisle."

Pike started as if he had been stung. "Somewhere between—— What are you talking about, sir? . . . Isn't he here? Isn't he over at Polferry?"

Anthony shook his head. "No. He left rather hurriedly last night. He had, so I found out from his man when I called this morning, been summoned upon urgent business."

Lucas knocked the long ash from his cigar. "Urgent business, eh? Any idea what it is, Gethryn?"

Anthony allowed himself a smile. "I know exactly what it was. Dr. Hale-Storford left in a hurry because Dr. Hale-Storford had read in his London papers that Miss Susan Kerr was going to Scotland. Dr. Hale-Storford suddenly discovered that he, too, wanted to go to Scotland. And so he's gone."

Pike stared. "But—good Lord, sir! Oughtn't we——"

"No necessity. Miss Kerr's not really gone, Pike. The first day I got here, I wrote and told Heath to get the notice put in. I wanted to see whether it would have an effect on Hale-Storford and also get Hale-Storford out of the way. It did both."

"You can't prove that!" Lucas put in quickly. "And I don't suppose, if it comes to that, that you actually *know* he's gone to Scotland."

"My dear Lucas, of course I can't prove it; of course I don't *know* it! I can't prove *anything* in this damn hotch-potch of a business. Even what I'm going to show you to-night—" he looked out of the coffee-room window at the gathering dusk—"you'll tell me isn't proof. And it isn't. But it's such a circumstantial backing to conjecture that even the official mind will have to take notice of it."

And that was all they could get out of him

just then. He would talk—and did—upon any subject other than this one nearest their minds. They gave it up after a bit, having to be satisfied with the one reasonable statement they had had from him.

"I am going," he had said, "to take you for a nice drive in my new motor . . . when it's dark. Everything looks so weird and nice, don't you think, under the headlights. . . ."

(5)

"Old Nick's Corner," said Anthony over his shoulder. The big car checked; swung round a bend so acute that when once more it ran straight it was going back almost parallel with the way it had come.

Lucas clutched at the top of the door. "Old Nick's driving!" he muttered to Pike. "Damn it, man, d'you like this?" He turned his head, peering at his companion through the soft, thick darkness.

Pike's shrug Lucas felt rather than saw. Pike's voice said:

"Well, sir, he never *has* had a smash!" There

was an undercurrent in the tone which suggested little faith in the continuance of this clean sheet.

Lucas leant forward. He said into Anthony's ear:

"Easy, Gethryn. Go easy!"

Anthony did not turn his head. But his voice showed surprise. "My dear chap! Only doing forty-five or so."

The great head lamps cut before their progress a path of impossible whiteness. But on each side of the spreading swath of brilliance was darkness blacker, thought Anthony's passengers, than any darkness has right to be. The near side obscurity was nothing to them. They knew, from the flashes of light the great lamps gave them at the many curving corners, that upon this side lay the comparative safety of rock and bramble. . . . But the other side! Of that side they had only, because of the angles of these turns, only had two glimpses. But these had been enough and more than enough. Upon their right was . . .

"Nothing!" Lucas muttered. "And a great

deal of it, going down the devil of a long way!"

The car purred on. And up. Its hundred horsepower made light of the twisting, ever-steepening ascent. And always upon their right Anthony's passengers felt that blankness, that ever increasing void.

"Where the hell's he taking us?" Lucas's voice hid perturbation beneath assumed ill-patience.

Again Pike's half felt shrug. "This is the west road up to the Tor top, sir. The Long Road they call it . . . And rightly, I'd say! We come out just above Polferry itself, sir."

"If . . ." said Lucas. "God! Easy, Gethryn!" The car, to take a particularly sharp left-hand bend, had swung its great nose first outward to the right. The white shadow-pitted ribbon of road had for an instant become part of the blackness. The lights' beam had gone out, a full quarter mile, into—void.

"Right!" came Anthony's voice. The car swung left. The road came back again, and the rock and bramble. The night air, almost cold now at this height, fanned Lucas's face. He

sighed and put up an unsteady hand to a forehead which was frigidly damp.

Pike let out pent breath in a little hissing
whistle. He said:

"*Think* we're at the top now, sir."

The car slackened, drew smoothly to a standstill. Anthony turned in his seat. They saw his
face as a faint blur. It said:

"We are." He made a gesture. "You are now,
gentlemen, upon the plateau of Polferry Hill.
Or Tor. If you could see, you could see for miles
in any direction." Another half-seen gesture.
"You could see, for instance—over there—the
main Exeter–London road. It joins this road
about a quarter of a mile ahead of us. And about
another two hundred yards on, past the join, a
steep hill, a very steep hill, runs down to Polferry and the sea. At the end of that steep hill
is the Watch House."

"I wish I knew——" Lucas never finished
this sentence. The car started, not with a jerk
but with a smooth, enormously accelerating
rush, which left him, for the moment, actually

without breath and imaginatively without insides.

It slowed down again, dropped from nearly a mile a minute to less than half that pace. Anthony spoke from the driving seat:

"There, just to your left, that's where the London–Exeter road joins on. Along it, some months ago, came Miriam Rossiter driving her own car alone. She was going down to see her dead sister's husband. She was late. She was always a fast driver." The car slowed still further. Now it could not have been doing more than fifteen miles an hour. Anthony turned to end this speech. He said over his shoulder: *"We are now Miriam Rossiter. Get me?"*

He did not wait for answer. He turned, settled himself back in his seat, and put his right foot down. When the needle on the speedometer dial touched 55 he held the car at that pace.

The head lights now showed the road as a broad white river. The big engine was so silent that only the scream of new tires on the macadam surface spoilt the silence. Anthony said suddenly:

"Three hundred yards ahead on the road is the beginning of Polferry Hill." His voice carried faintly to the back seat.

Lucas turned to say something to Pike; thought better of it; held his tongue.

Pike said: "He's going to go past it!"

Anthony was not. Anthony did not. Fifty yards from the turn, he began to brake; had slowed the car at the turn sufficiently to take the turn. As the front wheels came straight again, his voice came to the passengers' ears once more. It said:

"Don't forget. *We are Miriam Rossiter.* We are alone. We are a fast woman driver, and we know this hill. Hang on a bit."

"Oh, my *God!*" said Lucas.

The car, at first, seemed to drop like a plummet. This was a hill—and a steep one—and its steepness after the first two hundred yards was not straight but winding. Hugging the left of the road, Anthony let the great car almost have her head. He put out a hand and turned out the switch which lit the dashboard. Pike, who had been straining to see the speed, sank back with

a little grunt. He found himself clutching the
door on the off side just as Lucas was clutching
the door on the near. The car swayed a little at
the turns; otherwise it held magically to the
bumpy road.

Lucas had not been down this road before.
Pike had. It is to be guessed that Pike suffered
the more. For while Lucas's fear came atop of
and after each hazard, Pike's fears were constant both for hazard past and hazard to come.

There is, halfway down Polferry Hill, a
sharp bend to the left followed by a slow curved
bend to the right—a most dangerous piece of
road. On the left a bank topped by curious little
stunted trees rears up to a height of thirty feet
or more. On the right, a ridiculously fragile single post and rail fence—rotten with age—is the
only barrier between the road and an almost
sheer drop to the coombe below.

Anthony slowed for this, but he did not slow
much. Not enough for Lucas. Lucas abandoned,
for one instant, his grip upon the door, leaned
forward and touched the driver upon the shoulder.

"Gethryn! . . . Gethryn! . . ." he said, "for God's sake, man, slow down!"

But Anthony did not slow down. His voice came:

"Shut up! *We are Miriam Rossiter.*" He went on.

The slope increased, and he had to brake. The car was sliding down the hill at something between forty and fifty miles an hour. His pressure upon the brake pedal increased. He slid, with a creditable lack of noise, into third gear; took his foot from the brake pedal. The speed, as well indeed it might, decreased. Still the bank towered upon their left. Still the rotting fence marked the drop upon the other side of the barely twenty-five-foot roadway. The lights cut a white highway through the darkness. In the back seat Pike was breathing heavily; Lucas cursing softly between his teeth. . . .

Another turn. Another steeper drop. Another turn. A noticeable decrease of steepness once more. The car is in top gear. Once more accelerating. Then Anthony's voice again, louder this time:

"Two turns now and then the Watch House wall. As soon as it begins, think *'Rossiter'*."

Between his curses, which were, as curses so often are, really prayers, Lucas found time to speak to his companion. He said in a whisper, which sought to disguise its gasping origin:

"What's he playing at?"

No answer: with a sudden swerve, first to the right, then once more to the left, they were running under the lee of the wall of which they had been warned. The wall of the garden of the Watch House. It ran parallel with the road, grimly replacing the bank which had been upon their left until now. Part of the hard-cut flood of light from the lamps showed it to them along its length. They saw suddenly, only a few yards ahead of them, yet another bend. The wall swung left, and with it, following round it at a more obtuse angle, the road. A blind corner, if ever there was one.

"*Rossiter,*" called Anthony.

He slackened the car's speed, but only a little. She must have been travelling at nearly forty. He hugged the left, nosed out a little for the turn, then, with a hard wrench of his wheel, took it. . . .

"Oh, God! . . . ."

Lucas's voice was a shout, almost a shriek. Pike rose in his seat until he was standing, then fell back into it. His breath left him in a gasp . . . .The roadway narrowed here, and rushing toward them at a pace terrific was another car; the blaze of its headlights blinded them. They could not see. They felt already the beginnings of that lurch with which, if their driver did the only thing a driver could do and swung out right-handed, they would crash through that single rail and go over and down into the coombe. Lucas flung up an arm to cover his eyes. Pike's head was already almost on his knees. . . .

Anthony's voice: "Well, I said *'Think Rossiter'.*"

The car came to a standstill so abruptly that both its passengers found themselves upon their knees.

"I said *Rossiter,*" came Anthony's voice again. "You know you don't trust me."

Pike, the first of the pair to regain full control, got to his feet. He stood, his mouth open in amazement, clutching the back of Anthony's seat. Over Anthony's head, over the windscreen, he stared at the car which had nearly been their death. It had stopped not more than two feet from them. Still its head lights blazed into his eyes. It was a big car. A big black open car foreshortened by his end-on view of it. There was a man in the driving seat—and something in the back. What was it? A man standing just as he was standing looking over his head at him just as he was looking over Anthony's head at the man. . . .

Suddenly he saw.

"Well, I'm goshed!" he said. He bent down. He shook Lucas by the shoulder. "Have you seen, sir? Have you seen?"

Lucas, not standing, but peering out as he sat, nodded feebly. "Yes! What is it? What the hell is it?"

"Us, sir!" Pike's nerves found relief in a hoarse cackling little laugh. "Us, sir. It's a blooming mirror!"

"Well, I'm . . ." Lucas said what he was: it is to be doubted whether anyone had ever heard him more British.

Now Anthony was out of the car and standing in the road. He was saying, impatience in his tone: "Come on! Come on! I want you to look at this."

They came on. Pike, fully recovered, with agility. Lucas with not even pretence at speed. When he came up to them, some nine feet in front of the car's bonnet, he found them examining a great mirror in which the glare of the car's lights was now obliterated by their own bodies.

It was a great mirror in an oaken frame. It seemed, at first sight, to be standing upright without support. Lucas blinked; looked again; found it to be supported from above. Its left-hand edge, as he faced it, was almost against the wall, and at that point in the wall was a gap; a gap some two feet wide and five in depth, reducing thereby the head of the wall within itself from eleven feet to six. Through this gap, out into the road, at a height of six

feet from the ground was thrust a limb of ash
and it was to this limb that the top edge of the
mirror was fixed, so that the mirror was held
four inches off the ground and six inches out
from the wall more than halfway across the
very narrow road.

Lucas frowned. Anthony and Pike were talking, but he was not yet in mood to join them.
He was trying, instead, to puzzle things out for
himself. He had not got far when he was made
to join the conversation. Anthony turned. He
drew a torch from his pocket; shone the torch's
beam across the narrow road toward the rickety,
foolish fence which guarded the precipice. He
said:

"Well, look there! That's where she went.
Lucas, have a look at this."

Lucas joined them. Along the white beam of
the torch he looked. He saw that immediately
opposite where he was standing, almost directly
facing, that is, the gap in the wall from which
came the bough which supported the mirror,
was a section of fencing whose newness was in
glaring contrast to the rest.

"That," said Anthony, "they did a fortnight after the Rossiter woman went over. Straight there, she went, and straight down. The car must have turned over about six times, but she was still inside it. Come over here and look." He took three strides and was at the rail. He bent over it, shining his torch downward. They followed him slowly. They stood one on each side of him, craning over. The torch was a powerful torch, but its beam did not show them, they could tell, the half nor the quarter of that drop. Not quite a sheer drop, but perhaps all the worse for that. Anthony sent the beam casting this way and that. It flickered; came to a stand which showed, twenty feet down the steepness below them, a broken sapling with half its root in air, the other half precariously clinging to earth. He said:

"She hit that and then went on." He suddenly snapped off the torch's beam and turned.

Lucas was himself again. He said:

"What's all this, Gethryn? Do I get what you seem to be trying to tell us, or am I mad?"

"You'll see soon enough." Anthony's voice

was savage and pitched very low. "Quiet now, and just follow me. Not much of a climb."

Lucas groaned. "My *God!* What are we in for now?" He thought he was making this remark to Pike, but found that he was not. Pike, on Anthony's heels, was already at the gap. Through it went Anthony. Then Pike. Lucas struggled after; found himself, after a painful, hand-scraping descent—the ground on the other side of the wall was lower by far than he had expected—standing ankle deep in leaf mould and loam. He looked about him, blowing upon his scorched palms. He became aware, with the shock a man will get when he realizes that there has been something near him for many moments that he has not seen, that he was standing almost immediately beneath a gaunt and darkly towering mass. He craned his neck to peer up at it. It seemed to his jolted and disordered mind like a giant's tripod camera. The legs of the tripod he could see, but the mass atop of them he could only guess at. He moved instinctively closer to his companions. He said, in a voice whose steadiness did him credit:

"Where are we, Gethryn? Pinch me, will you? I think I must be asleep or something."

"Quiet!" came Anthony's voice. "Don't want the Great Danes at you, do you? I don't, anyhow."

Lucas dropped his voice to a whisper. "What *is* this? Where are we?"

"Watch House grounds. That—" in the darkness Anthony's arm made a gesture— "that's what they call the Tower. We're going up there. Now, quiet, for God's sake!"

He turned from them. He put a hand up to his mouth. A little plaintive whistle like the sound of a bird disturbed made a soft hole in the silence of the night.

Beside him Lucas felt Pike suddenly stiffen. "What's that?" he said.

Anthony turned on them. "Quiet, will you! Only White." A shape came out from between the legs of the giant's tripod. Its feet made soft rustlings on the mouldering carpet. It came close to them, a stocky, thickset figure. A dim gesture in the darkness showed it to be touching its cap. It did not speak.

"Good work, White," said Anthony. "Now we'll get the props back. Bear a hand, Pike, will you?"

Lucas was left standing. The three went from him back toward the gap in the wall. He barely heard them. After a small pause he did hear them. They were coming back. They were carrying between them something large and flat which, catching such light as there was, sent out faint gleams. They came level with him and set down the mirror flat upon its back.

"Get that bough off again, White." Anthony's voice was very low, almost a whisper.

White, taking something from his pocket, knelt. There came, separated at thirty second intervals, three separate creakings. Then White's voice: "What will I do with the bough, sir?"

"Where you found it," said Anthony, "and then stay down here. We're going up. If you hear anything, whistle. . . . Come on, you two."

He led them straight into the blackness encompassed by the tripod's legs; out again the other side and there turned sharp to his right.

They were now at the end of a flight of wooden steps. Anthony led the way. He said, his foot on the first stair:

"'Ush, 'ush, I will 'ave 'ush."

They followed after him, treading like cats. They came up, after a climb whose caution and precariousness took from him much of Lucas's recovered breath, onto a wooden platform. Before them loomed a bulk like an enormous beehive. Lucas could see now, but only dimly, what the giant's camera really was. Opposite Anthony there was a door. He set his fingers to the handle. There came the click-click of a lock giving, and then his whisper to their ear. They followed.

The beam of his torch shone out again; went flickering round.

"Just a minute!" he said. Then the splutter of a match and after it the faint, increasing light of an oil lamp.

Lucas and Pike, now beyond all amazement, looked around them. They were in a great hexagonal chamber. The heavy shutters lining five of the six sections of wall were shutters of windows; the sixth section was wooden wall distempered over. They stood upon a plain thick piled carpet which stretched over the whole of the floor space. They saw a vast desk and armchair before it; other chairs; a table or two and, for the rest, bookshelves. Anthony went to the centre table and picked up the lamp. Held it above his head.

"Yes," he said, "the workroom, study—call it what you like—the place, anyhow, of Dr. Hale-Storford. Moved his things here to work after his wife's death. Couldn't, quite reasonably, stand his own study in the house. Likes this. View's good. So it ought to be. This wooden thing was built by the last tenant on the site of the old Watch Tower in the estuary mouth. . . . Well, got there? Dr. Hale-Storford's workroom. Moved his stuff into it—get your teeth into this—exactly a fortnight after his wife's death. Still lived in the house. Always worked here. Does still. Now look!" He went, still carrying the lamp above his head, across to the one section of wall. They followed after him, Pike with two eager strides, Lucas more slowly. They stood at his shoulder. With his free hand he pointed.

"See that? See that discolored square there? Those two great nails? That's where the mirror hangs. The mirror that White's standing beside at this moment. It's been up here ever since Hale-Storford had the room furnished. Three weeks after he'd had the room furnished, that is, about five weeks after his wife's death, there was a gale. A big ash, which you may or may not have seen lying there as you came through the gap, was blown down and smashed the wall. Hale-Storford, sitting up here every day, brooding, must've seen the gap every time he looked out of *that* window. I can feel the idea coming to him, can't you? Lonely road. . . . His suspect driving down it, as she always did, too fast. . . . Dark night. . . . What would happen if, just as she comes round the corner before that gap hugging the wall because of the narrowness of the road, she was suddenly to see what looked like another car rushing at her? What would she do? First she'd brake. Then see that braking was useless. Then, when she saw that the other car was still hugging the wall, she would, almost at the last moment, desperately wrench her wheel over to the right in the dim hope of passing the oncoming car on its off and her near side. But the road is so narrow that the hope doesn't come off. She hits that rotten bit of fencing and down she goes. . . ."

A long low whistle came from Pike. "That's about it, sir. But how, in the name of Jing, did you first hit on the idea?"

Anthony walked back to the table and set down the lamp. He said:

"Not so difficult, you know. You see, following my normal practice, I was prejudiced to begin with. I believe—you could almost say I knew—that Hale-Storford had been the author of this accident. Therefore I'd only got to say to myself *how* was he the author of this accident? I drove slowly down that road in the daytime. As soon as I saw the gap in the wall which is almost dead opposite the place where the Rossiter woman went over, I naturally connected gap with smash. I thought, at first, that through that gap he'd done something to scare

her—flashed a great light; made a faked
obstruction—anything like that. A dozen ideas
or more. But I found that none of them was
really sure enough. I thought: What would
make an experienced driver take the awful risk
of swerving out there? The answer, the most
satisfactory answer, was another car going the
other way on its wrong side. I began to make
inquiries about other cars as best I could. I
found first, through the servants via White,
that neither Hale-Storford's own big car nor
what had been his wife's small car had left the
garage on the night that Miriam Rossiter was
killed. I also found that all that day Hale-
Storford had been at home. He hadn't left the
house, or at least he hadn't left the grounds.
This car, this possible car to frighten Miriam
Rossiter off the road, was therefore, not one of
his cars and couldn't have been any other car
driven by him. Therefore, again, it was probable that Miriam Rossiter's death wasn't caused
by another car. Yet another car was the best
solution. . . . I got a bit gummed up there, I
must say. And then I discovered that this place

we're standing in now wasn't derelict but used. On principle, I had a look at it. I did it by daylight. It wasn't a very pleasant job, because I might have been seen from the house at any moment. However, I'd a chance, as Hale-Storford at least wasn't at home. The first thing I saw when I got in here was that mirror. It's a big thing, you know, rather an unusually big one. . . . I looked at it. I looked at it for a long time. Then in my mind I saw the gap, and after I'd seen the gap, I saw the whole thing.

"I took the mirror down. Through the top of the frame I found recent and unaccounted for nail holes. I also found, sticking to the rough wood at the back of the frame, fragments of fibre which turned out to be bark. I remembered all those great ash boughs lying about just below. I saw the whole thing." He broke off suddenly and turned to Lucas.

"Sorry about that drive," he said.

"How," said Lucas sourly, "do you look when you're pleased?"

Anthony grinned. "Never mind. It was the

best way to convince you. It *did* convince you, didn't it?"

Lucas nodded without speaking.

"And now," said Anthony, "what about Hale-Storford? Will you or will you not have him officially watched? I know this isn't really evidence, but is it enough to make you look for real evidence? It *must* be, Lucas!"

Lucas nodded. "It is." He stood in the centre of the room looking about him. He said slowly:

"One thing. How the devil did he get that great glass down and then up again. Not a one-man job."

Anthony contradicted. "It is a one-man job. It's been done by one man to-night. In a moment I'm going to whistle, and you'll find that within three minutes White's back again with the glass and inside another two has it up again. You see, it's not a rigid frame. It folds."

"Specially made, sir?" Pike put in.

Anthony shook his head. "Not a bit of it. I should say it's a fairly old mirror made for a very large dressing table. It's quite solid work. And Pike, I don't think the desirability of killing Miriam Rossiter made Hale-Storford think of the mirror but that the mirror made him think of the best way of getting rid of Miriam Rossiter. That's sure, Pike."

He stopped abruptly and with four strides was at the door. He opened the door. A little breeze came coolly in. In the lamp light, Pike and Lucas looked at each other. From just outside there came to their ears once more the sound of that plaintive triple-note whistle.

CHAPTER SEVEN

LUCAS'S telephone buzzed angrily. Lucas, standing by the window looking out over the sunlit Thames, nodded toward the instrument. "See who that is, Pike."

Pike was at the table in a long stride; picked up the telephone. "Yes? . . . Yes." He looked up and said: "Colonel Gethryn, sir. Tell them to send him up?"

"Of course! Of course!" Lucas's tone was impatient. "I've told them about that before."

There was silence until the opening of the door. Anthony was with them. He was gay this morning; he gave gay greetings. Lucas surveyed his smartness with a jaundiced eye.

"Pleased with life, aren't you?" he said. "Why, exactly?"

Anthony grinned. He sat himself upon his favourite window sill and lit a cigarette.

"Well, Police." he said, "what's doing?"

Pike looked at Lucas; had his unspoken question answered with a nod. He went to Lucas's table, took from it an envelope and from the envelope folded buff sheets of foolscap. He gave these to Anthony.

"I think, sir," he said, "you'd best read that for a start."

Anthony read:

"RICHARD HALE–STORFORD

"Accordance with instructions, proceeded Edinboro by train 20th inst. Discovered at station Edinboro sleeper booked Hale-Storford's name by midnight train returning London. Waited station, found subject on train. Followed, picking up subject again at St. Pancras morning 21st inst.

"Subject proceeded Doulton's Hotel, Norfolk Street, S. W. Booked single room with bath, stated was staying two or three days, booking in own name.

"4 P. M. same day (21st inst.) subject left hotel, chartering taxicab. Followed in another cab. Subject drove to offices of the Thameside-Carringspey Steamship Company. Stayed outside offices while subject was within, subsequently followed subject back to Doulton's Hotel. Reported Inspector Fox and accordingly handed over outside Doulton's Hotel to D. O. Bryce. Self proceeded back to steamship offices. Inquiries elicited that subject had booked passage to Carringspey for night sailing of 22d inst. on S. S. *Sheila McNab*. Booking was for two, with adjoining cabins. Subject gave name John Garratt. Subject stated to shipping clerk that he was taking invalid daughter to Scotland for health. Must have adjoining cabins, as daughter required constant attention. Booking was made and fee paid by subject in Bank of England £1 notes.

"S. S. *Sheila McNab* sails from Grafton Docks 8:15 P. M. 22d inst.

"Returning to Doulton Hotel relieved D. O. Bryce. Booked room in Hotel for self on same landing as subject. Subject had been in room since return from shipping offices and continued in room until 6:30, when descended and sat in lounge reading.

"(Regret to report that owing to possibility of telephone in subject's room having escaped my notice, did not check up on telephone calls. Discovered later that subject had telephoned; call having been put through to Polferry 10. Unable obtain any information in regard purport of call.)

"Subject did not leave hotel at all, retiring to

bed at 10:30. Kept subject's room under observation throughout night; subject did not leave.

"Telephoned Inspector Fox this morning and at 9:30 handed over again to D. O. Bryce, returning to make report herewith.

P. Strangways,

D. O. (C. I. D.) 342.

June 22, 193–.

Anthony folded up the buff sheets. He said, looking first at Lucas, then at Pike:

"So Mr. Garratt and his invalid daughter are going to Scotland. Well, well! What about the invalid daughter, Lucas?"

Lucas frowned. He was plainly disturbed this morning. He said, after a pause:

"Point Pike and I were discussing when you came in. So far we haven't had Miss Kerr watched. Heath's been doing that himself. But now . . ."

Anthony nodded. "Exactly! Well, we don't want, do we, to frighten the doctor off altogether?"

Pike brightened at this. "Just what I was saying, sir." He looked at Lucas apologetically, then back at Anthony. "If I may say so, sir, what Mr. Lucas and I were suggesting was to leave Miss Kerr as she is, only to warn Captain Heath and herself that she's not to leave the house to-day. After all, clever as he may be and mad as he may be, this Hale-Storford can't go into a house and pull her out of it, can he?"

Lucas turned from blank-eyed contemplation of the river. He said:

"I don't like this case. It's a mess." His tone was petulant.

"I think," said Anthony, "what Pike said is right. If we scare Hale-Storford off, we may never get him. We've got nothing yet that would go against him in court, you know, Lucas."

"Do I *know!*" Lucas was almost shrill. "That's the devil of it. . . . All right! Pike, can you get onto Captain Heath?" Pike nodded. "Do it, then, and do it now. Just tell him that Miss Kerr's not to go out of the house to-day. You can tell him also that his job of looking after her will be taken over by us from seven o'clock to-night."

He stopped here to look at Anthony. "We'd better do that, Gethryn. If he's going to try and get her, it'll be before that, won't it?"

Anthony nodded. "Yes, sound move. After seven put a man on, if you like. Plain clothes. Obvious or not. Up to seven, leave it alone."

Pike nodded; was gone. The door shut softly behind him. Lucas walked from the window back to his chair; sat and stared at Anthony.

"There's a thing," he said, "I meant to ask you when we were down at Morlock. Who's in that house of Hale-Storford's now? You said something about servants."

Anthony nodded. "Yes. Two servants—man and wife—and of course Dorothy Graye, house-keeper."

Lucas frowned, twisting uneasily in his chair. "Yes, I thought you'd say that. That Graye woman. . . . Look here, Gethryn, has another possible solution of this business occurred to you?"

Anthony smiled. "Yes. The one you're just going to put forward."

For a moment Lucas lost his frown. "You say

it first, then," he said; "otherwise glory's easy."

"After all these years," said Anthony sadly, "you still don't trust me! Listen, what you were going to suggest was that Dorothy Graye was the killer of Eve Hale-Storford, and that she was the killer of Eve Hale-Storford with Richard Hale-Storford's knowledge. That right?"

Lucas smiled; a little wryly. "Blast you!" he said, "it is. What's the matter with it, anyhow?"

It was Anthony's turn to frown. "Tell you the truth, I don't know, but it's not right. Don't fit. For one thing, if Graye killed Mrs. Hale-Storford with Hale-Storford's knowledge, why this elimination holocaust?"

"Accidents," said Lucas. His voice was very low, almost ashamed. "Pure coincidental accidents."

"My *dear* chap! What about Mr. John Garratt and his invalid daughter and their nice little holiday in Scotland?"

"Easy," said Lucas, but he did not sound it. "Doctor Hale-Storford has a lady friend, and that'd be a nice quiet way of getting his lady friend up to a nice quiet country for a pleasant week or so."

Anthony nodded. "Ingenious . . . but it won't wash, Lucas, and you know it won't. You're uncomfortable about it. You don't believe it yourself. Do you, now?"

With an impatient gesture Lucas threw down the pencil he had been holding. He got up, thrusting his chair savagely back. He said:

"No, I don't. If you want to know, I don't believe anything in this business. And one of the things I find it hardest of all to believe is that we've had three deliberate murders and haven't got one tittle of evidence that'd be a ha-porth of good in a court. Look here, Gethryn, suppose we do find that Hale-Storford is mad, as you say; that he's what you call eliminating possible murderers of his wife; suppose, in other words, we catch him to-day trying to make Miss Kerr into John Garratt's invalid daughter. . . . Then we know and he knows. But how the devil are we going to *prove* it?"

"Ask me," said Anthony, "another! But once

get your hooks into him and you may at least be able to prove he's mad, and in any case, you could get him several years for abduction."

Lucas snorted. "Several years for abduction! When the man ought to be hanged twice! What's the good of that?"

Anthony's smile was sympathetic. "Unsatisfactory, I know, but the good of it is, Lucas, that we take a young and very charming girl out of danger. That we put an end to the possibility of there being other 'accidents.'"

"Oh, I know all that!" Lucas was pacing savagely up and down his carpet. "I know all that, but it's all so . . ."

"The official mind," said Anthony, *"in excelsis!* You know, Lucas, what you'd really like would be to get the Kerr girl nicely killed and have Scotland Yard officers taking photographs of Hale-Storford while he killed her. You'd then have a nice tidy case against him. It seems to be a rooted idea that policemen are for shutting stable doors. I think they ought to be for seeing that the horses are tied up properly."

Lucas stopped in his walking. Lucas glared at Anthony.

"If you think," he said, "that I——"

Anthony's smile cut him short. Anthony said, looking at his watch:

"It's half-past twelve. A bit early, but still . . . You come out with me and have some lunch. That's what you want, largely liquid."

(2)

Once more Lucas and Pike and Anthony were in Lucas's room. The swift-dropping sun cut a gilt path across the dull carpet. The clock upon Lucas's desk stood at five minutes before seven. They were silent; Lucas and Anthony smoking, Pike looking reflectively at the shining toecaps of his boots.

Lucas stirred. "What time was it we start, Pike?"

Pike looked up quickly. "Half an hour, sir. Just about twenty past seven. I've ordered the car for then. I'm taking two men and you and Colonel Gethryn. We go straight to the Docks." His tone showed a barely controlled eagerness.

The prospect of action, even after years of service in this most active of professions, always excited him.

Anthony stood up; flung a cigarette stub across the room and into the empty grate. "To meet," he said, "John Garratt and daughter. Well, well!"

The telephone buzzed. Lucas tilted forward his chair, reached forward a long arm; spoke:

"Yes? Who? . . . He's what? . . . *What!* Send him up at once, man, at once!"

He stared, the receiver still in his hand, at his companions. He put the receiver back. He said slowly:

"Heath's downstairs. Murphy says 'in a state.' Something about Miss Kerr."

Anthony's eyebrows went up. Pike jumped to his feet, and crossed with long strides to the door. He left it wide behind him. They heard his quick footsteps crossing the outer office, and then, as he reached that door and opened it, the sound of other footsteps in the corridor outside, and voices. . . .

And then he was with them again. Behind

him there came Heath. Heath, though he was not speaking, whose white, drawn face and blazing eyes brought Lucas and Anthony simultaneously to their feet. It was to Anthony that Heath spoke. He said, his voice low and straining for steadiness:

"She's gone!"

No sound from Pike. From Lucas:

"What! What's that you say?"

From Anthony, coming forward:

"Here, man, sit down!"

He pushed a chair forward with his words. Its edge took Heath behind the knees and he fell into rather that sat in it. Anthony said, looking at him:

"When?"

From his breast pocket Heath pulled a handkerchief, passed it once across his brow. "Somewhere," he said, "between five and six-thirty."

"How?"

"God knows!" Heath's voice was beginning to rise. His teeth bit his underlip. He swallowed; controlled himself. He said:

"I'd made her see reason. She wasn't going

out. *I* went out, bloody fool that I am! Went out at quarter to five; said I'd be back in another two hours. She wasn't to move. I went to my father's house. I was just leaving there——"

"Time?" said Anthony.

"About six. I was just going when the phone bell went. It's in the hall. My father's man answered it. The call was for me. It was from St. Adrian's Hospital. . . ."

"Hammersmith?" asked Anthony.

"Yes. The house surgeon was speaking. Doctor something—I didn't catch his name. He said there'd been a motor accident in Hammersmith Broadway, that a Miss Susan Kerr had been very seriously injured and kept asking for me. . . ."

The handkerchief again. This time the man wiped his lips as well as his brow. He said jerkily, for his breath was coming in barely controlled gasps:

"She was barely conscious, they said, but kept asking for me. Could I please arrange to go there at once. I should—I should, of course,

have rung you first, but I don't know why—
except I'm a damn fool not fit to be trusted—it
never entered my head—nothing entered my
head except Susan. My father's car was just
outside the door. I just pelted out of the house,
jumped into the car, and drove to Hammersmith."

He broke off again. Once more the handkerchief. He said, after a fight for composure all
the more distressing to watch by reason of its
restraint:

"Of course, when I got to the hospital they
knew nothing about it. Nothing at all. . . . I
saw what had happened. I got back into the car
and went to Susan's house quicker even than I
had driven to the hospital. When I got there . . .
You can guess, I suppose."

"Mean she'd gone?" said Lucas.

"Shut up!" Anthony was savage. "What did
they know, Heath? At the house, I mean."

Heath shook his head. Rather a painful sight;
he forgot to stop shaking it. He said:

"Nothing. Only one of the servants had seen
her go. A telephone message had come for her,

and she'd answered the telephone. After that she'd said nothing to anyone, but they saw her go upstairs and come down a few moments later dressed for the street. She seemed, they said, very white. There was no one in the hall actually when she came down. She must have let herself out. All they could tell me was that a parlourmaid who happened to be in the dining room saw Susan go down the steps, saw her look this way and that, saw a taxi pull up and Susan get into it."

He swallowed twice and endeavoured to clear his throat. "That's all," he said hoarsely. The whole man seemed to slump with these last words. Huddled in the big chair, he looked half his size. Pike looked at Lucas; got an answering nod; was gone from the room.

Anthony put a hand on the sagging shoulder. He said:

"It's all right, man. It's all *right!* We know where. We're going soon. At once. You can come too."

Into Heath's body life seemed to flow back visibly. He stood erect. His shoulders squared themselves. He said, with rather a dreadful eagerness:

"You *know?* Tell me! Tell me!"

Anthony told him. At the end of the telling Pike was in the room again. He had in his right hand a glass. He held it out to Heath.

"Drink that, sir," he said.

Heath stood up. He took the glass and swallowed the contents at a single gulp. "Thanks," he said.

They were all standing now.

"Car right, Pike?" came Lucas's voice.

"Yes, sir."

"Men there?"

"Yes, sir."

Lucas looked at Anthony. "All set, Gethryn?"

Anthony nodded. . . .

They filed out. The room was empty.

(3)

The closed blue police car shot along the Embankment at speed. Behind it always, almost as if an invisible twenty-foot chain were coupling the two, was Anthony's Voisin-Maxwell.

In the police car were Lucas and Pike and two plain-clothes men. In Anthony's car were its owner and Trevor Heath.

Out of the Embankment they went, and then plunged into the thoroughfares of the City. In the police car there was silence but at Anthony's side, Heath talked incessantly. His speech did not require answer. Anthony let him talk.

As they came into the Minories from Fenchurch Street Heath looked at his watch.

"Seven-thirty," he said. "Are we in time, man? Are we in time?"

Anthony nodded. "Plenty. Sailing's not until eight-fifteen."

Ahead of them the police car took a sharp left turn into East Smithfield. The Voisin-Maxwell swung round on its tail. A few hundred yards, and then sharp right into Nightingale Lane. Then more twists and turns. . . .

Heath, with this approach to the end of their journey, grew almost silent. Only every now and then, for an instant or so, when the police car was out of sight, did he speak. Then a halt.

Anthony shut off his engine and brought his car
to a standstill with its nose almost touching the
tail light of the blue saloon. Already Pike and
the two plain-clothes men were on the pavement, and Lucas was following. Heath swung
his legs over the Maxwell's low side, dropped
to ground, and rushed to join them. Anthony
came after. Pike was saying to the driver of
the police car:

"Stay here till we're back, Richards, and look
after Colonel Gethryn's car as well as this one."

The man touched his cap.

Pike said to Anthony: "Thought we'd best
stop here, sir. Less conspicuous, as it were, if
we walk. Only a step." He turned to the two
plain-clothes men. "You two drop behind," he
said, "until we're on the berth."

The little procession moved off. First Pike
and Lucas; then, a yard or two behind them,
Heath and Anthony; then, at a greater interval,
the two detectives.

Pike, who knew the dock district as well as
his own house, led them by a twisting short-cut

which seemed, as Heath said, to be never coming to an end. But it did end, and suddenly. They came out opposite the big main wooden gates of Grafton Dock. At the wicket Pike spoke softly to its guardian. The party passed through.

Anthony was silent. Heath, beside him, kept hitching up his sleeve to look at his watch. Once he seemed to lose restraint and began a sort of stumbling run. In two strides Anthony was up with him; had laid a restraining hand on his arm. "Steady there, man!" he said. "We're not going to let you down."

Heath passed a hand across his forehead. It came away glistening. He said:

"Sorry! But they're so slow. So *bloody* slow!"

Past berth after berth Pike led unerring way. Everywhere were soot and coal dust and grayness. Everywhere, towering to their right and to their left and to their front, were the masts and funnels of shipping. Every now and then, mournfully, a siren hooted. Every now and then, from everywhere came shrill whistles.

The party trudged on. Once more Anthony had to lay a steadying hand on Heath's arm. And then, at last, the halt.

"What's up?" said Heath. "What's the matter? Why are they stopping?"

Anthony pointed. Heath followed the finger's direction; saw in great black letters upon a board of grimy white the figures 18. At the moorings was a small, sturdy little passenger-tramp. Upon her bows, seen mistily through an oily veil of coal dust, were the words *Sheila McNab*.

It was Anthony's turn to look at his watch. The hands showed him that the time was ten minutes to eight. A foul, rickety gangway still stretched from the waist of the ship to the berth-side. Pike and Lucas spoke together in whispers. Lucas stood his ground, barring the way of the others. Pike ran up the gangway. Heath started forward, to be jerked to a standstill by Anthony's clutch at his coat. To Anthony he turned a face almost unrecognizable, gray-white, seamed and lined like an old man's, the blue eyes flaring from under the fair brows.

"Damn you!" he said. "Oh, *damn* you! Let me go."

"Easy, man!" Anthony's tone was curt. There was something in it which brought Heath back to sanity. He muttered something and was still.

Pike, now at the top of the gangway, was talking to a head which appeared to rest upon the bulwarks; a head fringed with gray beard and hair; a head surmounted by a dirty peaked cap several sizes too small for it. They saw the head shaking decisively, and then saw Pike put hand to pocket and bring out something over which the gray head pored; saw Pike, after this, turn toward them and beckon them on.

They went up the gangway: Lucas first, then Anthony with Heath hard upon his heels, then, at decent orderly distance, the two plain-clothes men. As the last of the party put foot upon the deck the gray beard was wagging at Lucas. From somewhere behind it came a bass and grumbling voice which said:

"Aye, twull be yon pairr. They're but now gone below. Fife's the cahbin."

A huge, spatulate, and completely black

thumb was jerked at the deck. "Wull I be showin' you?" said its owner. Lucas nodded.

The square bulk of the *Sheila McNab's* skipper went down the companion immediately before them. They stood, at last, in a group about him. He said, dropping his voice to a sibilant whisper of well-nigh incredible loudness: "Doorr yonder!" Once more the thumb was jerked. "That's the chiel. Lassie's next beyond."

Lucas muttered something. The old man stood aside. Past him Pike pushed. Anthony kept firm grip on Heath's arm. At the first door Pike knocked. No answer. He knocked again, louder. No answer. He tried the handle. He turned to look at them standing there in a huddled group behind him, a face from which the usual dark tan seemed to have paled. He said, looking at Lucas:

"Break it in, sir?"

Lucas nodded.

There was a violent wrench at Anthony's hand. Heath was gone. Heath, thrusting himself off like a leaping animal from the other side of the companionway wall, hurled himself at the door. It shivered and groaned but held.

Pike made a grab at him. "Back there a minute, sir, I'll do it."

But the man was beyond restraint. He thrust out an arm. Pike reeled back almost onto Lucas's feet. Heath leaped again. With a splintering crash the door gave. Headlong into the cabin he shot. They poured in after him. . . .

It was Pike and Anthony who, with their combined force, managed to lever the fingers of Heath from the throat of Hale-Storford.

Hale-Storford was flat upon his back on the floor. Upon his chest knelt Heath. In the cabin's one bunk, on a heap of bed linen, disordered and not too clean, lay a woman face downward and motionless. . . .

The little cabin was full of men. Pike, backing Heath into a corner, left him under Anthony's charge; turned to the two plain-clothes men. He pointed to the limp figure of Hale-Storford on the floor. "Take him outside," he said.

The taller of the two took the unconscious

man's shoulders; the other the feet. They shuffled out with their burden as emotionless, as unconcerned as if this they carried were a mattress.

Lucas was bending over the woman in the bunk. He had turned her to lie upon her back. He said now, over his shoulder:

"She's alive all right but I don't know what to make of her. Have a look, Gethryn."

With the last words he stood up and away from the bunk. The three men in the corner, Pike and Anthony with Heath between them, could not see the bunk. With a wrench Heath was free. He took half a step forward—then checked. With Lucas's word, "She's alive," a sudden flood of colour had come back to the ashen face, but now, once more, as if by an invisible sponge, that colour was wiped away. He stared. His mouth dropped open. He seemed to be trying to speak but could not. It was Pike who said, in a dazed whisper:

"*That's* not Miss Kerr!" He took two rapid steps and was at the bunk side. He looked down at the limpness, then turned. He said:

"That's Mrs. Graye!"

"My *God!*" said Heath. He sat down heavily upon the cabin's one chair. He put his elbows on his knees and buried his head in his hands.

Lucas, bewildered, looked at Anthony. The little place, so recently a shell of pandemonium, was filled now with utter silence.

Anthony broke it. He crossed with one long stride to the bunk, bent over the woman's limp body. Like Lucas, he felt the action of her heart. His fingers then sought her wrist and found the pulse, slow and perhaps a little faint, but regular. He bent above her face, his own close to it. He straightened, shaking his .head. He said to Lucas:

"Some dope I don't know. Can't smell anything. I should say she's all right."

"Can't bring a doctor here," said Lucas. "We must move her. This boat's sailing in ten minutes. Pike, slip along to that Old Man of the Sea and ask whether he's got a stretcher. As you go, tell Stenson and Coker to get their man off. . . ."

Five minutes later they were on the quay.

From the rail of the *Sheila McNab* a row of grimy, curious heads looked down. The dock-yard policeman came hurrying up; saluted. Pike took him aside. After talk Pike came back. He said:

"Ambulance just coming, sir. That'll take the lady. Hale-Storford can walk."

Lucas looked round. "Where've they taken him?" he said.

"Behind that shed, sir. Think you'd better come and see him. And you too, sir." He looked at Anthony. "It's on our way out."

"What are we *talking* for? God man, can't we hurry? Can't we hurry?" Heath, ever since his entry to the cabin, had been alternating silence with wild outbursts of speech.

Fifty yards away, round a corner of a long shed, appeared an ambulance. From it there came hurrying a round and bustling little figure with a black bag. Pike went to meet him; was back again after hurried speech. "This way, sir!" he said. "They'll look after the lady now."

He began to lead, almost running, back along the way they had come, when he reached the first long shed he stopped. They came up to him, Heath first, then Anthony, then Lucas. At the other side of the shed, seated on an upturned barrel, was Hale-Storford. Beside him, still stolid, still uninterested, were the two plain-clothes men.

"Look at that, just look at that!" Pike was saying.

A little faint whistle came from Anthony. Lucas was silent.

"My—*God!*" said Heath.

They had put handcuffs on Hale-Storford. He was hatless, and his blond hair was ruffled like an untidy child's. From under its thatch there peeped out upon the world two eyes which were overbright, overjoyful, overrestless. Like an animal's but not so sane.

Hale-Storford was pleased with his handcuffs. He held up his wrists, looking at the bright things round them this way and that. He shook his wrists so that the bright things jingled. And every time they jingled there came from his throat little chuckles of delight. The taller of the two guardians touched him on the shoulder. "Come on, now!" he said.

The bright eyes looked up at him; a bright smile lit the face. The blond tousled head was shaken mischievously. Once more the wrists were held in air and shaken. Again the jingling; again the chuckle. . . .

Lucas turned to Anthony. "Come on!" he said. "If I look at that I shall be sick."

Pike gave rapid orders. The taller of the two detectives nodded.

Heath jerked savagely at Anthony's arm. "Come on, man! Come on, for God's sake!"

They went on. Pike, frankly running now, led the way.

CHAPTER EIGHT

ONCE more Lucas's room was full and Lucas back again by his window. Anthony stood before the fireplace. Up and down the other side of the room paced Heath. Heath was saying:

"But who? Who? In the name of God, who?"

"For your own sake, Heath—" Anthony's tone was very even—"for your own sake take it quieter. We're not wasting time. They don't here, you know, however much it may seem like it. Pike'll be back in a minute."

With the words, Pike was. Before him he ushered a neatly dressed and more than neatly pretty girl of the superior domestic servant type. She was plainly nervous; equally plainly she had recently been weeping. Heath stared at her. "Good Lord!" he said. "Aren't you—aren't you . . .?"

"Yes, sir." The girl's voice was quivering still. "Please, sir, it was me that happened to see poor Miss Susan running out of the house this evening. Please, sir, what's happened to her?"

Pike brought a chair for the girl. He cut her short. "Now, now!" he said. "I've told you you're not to worry. You've got to help us, not cry." He was firm and yet benign.

"Y-y-y-yess, sir!"

"You just sit quietly there and keep hold of yourself. No need for you to talk just yet." He turned to Lucas and said:

"This is one of the parlourmaids at Lady Kerr's house, sir. The one that saw Miss Kerr leave this afternoon. She's already given me one very important piece of evidence. I brought her along here in case she might be wanted, sir. She just saw Miss Kerr run out of the house, look up and down the road—you correct me if I say anything wrong, my dear—and then run toward a taxi which was making, on the wrong side of the road, straight toward her. She looked through the window of the taxi, seemed to say something, and then wrenched open the door and got in. Miss Polton—that's this young lady's name—wasn't taking much notice, but she did happen to see all this. And then the taxi turned round and was off. What I've done is to put out a comb for all the taxi drivers round Brooke Square and district. If it's one of the regulars, we'll have him in and find out what he knows within an hour or two. If it's one—" he glanced at Heath, seemed about to stop, and then went on— "if it's one outside—floaters, we call them, Captain Heath—then it'll be a longer job. But you must remember that being a taxi makes it a help. If it had been one of the two million private cars, then things wouldn't have been so rosy."

"Rosy!" said Heath in a sort of barking laugh. *"Rosy!"* He flung himself into a chair and lay back, one hand pressed across his eyes.

Pike turned to Anthony. He said:

"Now for your line, sir. I've had Jackson ring up the Station at Morlock. He's had his answer already. Captain Banner's very well known down there. Hasn't left the town for more than six hours—and that in his boat—for the last six years. Still there."

Anthony nodded. "Thought so. Trenchard?"

Pike shrugged. "Jackson asked about that too, sir. This Mr. Trenchard was just staying for a week with Captain Banner at the time that Mrs. Hale-Storford was killed. Owing to the crime and his being in the house and having to wait for the inquest, he was there over two months. He left there, to be exact, on the thirtieth November last. Since when, sir—"

"—they've heard no other," Anthony finished.

"Exactly, sir."

"Pike— Lucas, can we ask Pike to get lines on Trenchard?"

Lucas stared. "Yes, yes. Anything. Pike, do what Colonel Gethryn asks."

"Yes, sir." Pike turned to Anthony.

Anthony, his eyes half closed, spoke quickly. He said:

"Get all Trenchard's particulars. You must have 'em from the inquest papers. Get onto every address and every possible address. Find out where he's been over these intervening six months or so. Find out his last known address. Get onto it. . . . You've got me, Pike? Anything and everything, and more than everything, about Trenchard. Keep Trenchard in your mind like a flag."

With long silent running strides Pike was gone from the room. The door banged behind him. In his chair Heath, striving for control, writhed his body about. In the middle of the room, upright upon a straight-backed chair, sat the girl Polton. Her eyes went this way and that. Her hands in their cheap, neat cotton gloves, twisted one about the other. Lucas sat upon the edge of his table and beat a little tattoo upon his teeth with the nail of his forefinger. Anthony stood where he was, back leaning against the mantelpiece, hands in his pockets.

Silence.

Suddenly Lucas swung to his feet, crossed to Anthony, said in a low voice:

"Why all this Trenchard, Trenchard, Trenchard? I see what you're driving at, but are you *sure?*"

Anthony shrugged. He said in a voice lower even than his questioners:

"What's sure in this world, Lucas? Nothing. But here's a thing that'll pass for sure. Take a life like Susan Kerr's. Is she likely to have been mixed up in a *lot* of things which would lead to attempts being made upon her life? What's the answer? A lemon. She isn't. But she *has* been mixed up in one thing, and out of that one thing we know that the 'accidents' sprang. Therefore it is—most *probably,* Lucas—out of the same thing that this abduction springs. Another separate thing would be stretching coincidence too far. I don't say it's impossible, because it isn't. Nothing's impossible. But we've got to deal with probabilities, Lucas. We're in a hurry. And out of that grisly house party—it *was* grisly, if you come to think of it—there's only one *possible* left, and that's Trenchard, if we except Banner working through understudies, which for our present purpose won't wash. It *must* be Trenchard we're after. Damn it, man, it's got to be!" He dropped his voice still lower. "Look at that poor devil in the chair there! Think of what he's going through. We've got to do something." Despite its lowness, his voice carried urgency greater than any Lucas had ever heard in it before.

Lucas nodded. "Yes, you're right. Damn you, man, you're always right!"

Anthony—his first sign of perturbation—raised his hand to his mouth; bit at his thumbnail. "I wish that was right."

"What?" asked Lucas.

"What you said."

Lucas drifted back to the table again, once more sat, once more began to beat out that barely audible devil's tattoo on his teeth. Still the girl Polton sat rigidly upright. Still her dark eyes darted their gaze from that face to this, from this face to the other. Still her hands were folded in her lap. In the armchair, almost facing her, lay Heath. His eyes were closed. His face showed dead-white against the dark leather of the chair. He was motionless, but even with this lack of movement and those closed eyes there was somehow something about the poise of the body—a tenseness, a sort of vibrant unseen urgency—which told you that this man was far from sleeping.

Moments passed, turned into minutes. Minutes became their quarter hour. Lucas, crushing out his fourth untasted cigarette, came back once more to the fireplace and Anthony. He said:

"Shall I ring for Pike? Been the devil of a time."

Anthony shook his head. "No, leave him. I would."

Now Lucas's left shoulder was brushing Anthony's right. They leaned, side by side, against the mantelshelf. Lucas turned his body. He said in a tone so low that it was really whispered:

"What do you think, Gethryn? Has this Trenchard been in it with that madman all the time?"

"God knows!" Anthony's voice too was a whisper. "I don't know what to think. And when I don't know what to think, I don't think. I'm not thinking."

"Where the hell," said Lucas, "has Pike got to?"

He was answered by the man himself. But Pike did not enter the room. Only his head came round the door. He looked at Lucas. "Just a minute, sir," he said. He looked at Anthony. "And you too, sir, if you would."

With one movement they left the fireplace and crossed to the door; passed through it. Pike said, very low:

"Nothing doing at all, sir. Can't get anything. This Trenchard—well, he seems like a ship without an anchor. Got plenty of strings on him, but they don't any of 'em lead anywhere. After he left Captain Banner he went back to his rooms at the Albany. He was there for eight or nine weeks, then he gave them up. Then he pops up in a new flat—he still rents it—in Vere Court, Westminster. He's there for another couple of months. Seems to have plenty of money. There's a man of his still there, but the man don't know where he is, or says not. Since then, nothing. Told the man he was going to Norway; all letters to be sent care of his bank in London, who'd forward them. Can't get the bank now; out of hours."

Lucas said sharply:

"This man, what is he? Valet?"

Pike nodded. "I should say so, sir. I've sent Bryce round there sharp. Maybe he'll have something when he comes back, but—" he shook his head, slowly this time— "somehow I don't feel he will, sir. My Gosh! This is a nasty business!"

"Anything in the taxi line, Pike?" This from Anthony.

Once more Pike's head was shaken. "No, sir. Nothing. Mind you, I never had much hope of that. What I said I said to try and cheer Captain Heath up. I'm not saying we shan't get anything, but we shan't get it all in a hurry like this."

Lucas made a little helpless gesture with shoulders and arms. He laughed; a sound with no mirth in it. He said:

"Looks like a stalemate."

Anthony began to walk up and down. "Stalemate hell!" he said.

"London—" said Pike— "well, London's a biggish place, sir."

"Scotland Yard," said Anthony, "is a biggish institution."

Lucas took fire. They were all on edge. Lucas said:

"And Scotland Yard's full of bloody fools! I know what you're thinking, Gethryn. Well, A. R. Gethryn's supposed to have a biggish brain. Suppose he does something about it!"

Pike looked from one to the other. His lean face, on top of its real distress, showed surface awkwardness at this bickering. Suddenly Anthony smiled.

"Sorry, Lucas, sorry! I asked for it!"

"Apologies," said Lucas, also with a smile, "returned. My fault! But what do we *do?*"

Anthony resumed his pacing. His footsteps sounded somehow slow and ominous. They watched him in silence. At last he came to a halt. He said:

"Let's try this girl. Let me try her. Send her out here. You two, if you don't mind, go back into the other room or somewhere else. Willing?"

"Aye, willing," said Lucas, and was gone.

Pike went after him. The door of Lucas's room closed behind them.

(2)

The girl came in. She said, a nervous, nearly hysterical shyness clouding her speech:

"You—they—please, sir——"

Anthony came forward; took her by the arm; settled her comfortably in the room's one comfortable chair, stood back from her and sat upon the table's corner. He said:

"Now, look here, Miss Polton . . ." then smiled. "That's a bit stiff, isn't it? What's your name?"

His tone was the right tone; a cunning blend of paternity, equality, interest, and friendliness. There came immediate signs of returning self-confidence. The dark eyes—in their way rather fine dark eyes—met Anthony's green ones fully. She said, and now she did not stammer:

"Elsie, sir," and then: "Oh, sir, isn't this dreadful about poor Miss Susan? If you only knew, sir, how——"

"I do, Elsie. I do. That's why I've asked to

have this talk with you. Now, looking at you
and talking to you, I know you'd do anything
for Miss Kerr, wouldn't you?"

"Oh, I would, sir!"

"And you don't dislike Captain Heath, do
you?"

"No, sir. We've— I've always thought that
the Captain and Miss Susan——"

"Exactly," said Anthony. "Exactly." His
smile and his tone were more than sufficient excuse for the interruption. He said, turning a
little as he sat:

"It seems to me, Elsie, that you're just the one
person in the world who *might* be able to help
us find Miss Kerr, and find her quickly. Mind
you, find her we shall, sometime or another,
whether you can help us or not, but what we
want to do, Elsie, for Miss Kerr's sake and for
Captain Heath's sake and for our own sakes, is
to find Miss Kerr now."

"Sir!" The girl's voice was eager, yet despair-
ing. "But, sir," she said again, "that other gentleman, what's his name, the police gentleman,
the one that came to the house, he asked me, and

I told him everything. Everything. You see, it wasn't as if I knew that Miss Susan oughtn't to 've gone out of the house. If I had, I might 've looked. I mean, I might have looked more specially like. As it was, well, I wasn't thinking, and it was just luck like that made me see anything at all. You see what I mean, sir?"

Anthony's smile was sympathetic. Very sympathetic. He pulled out a cigarette case. He said:

"Elsie, I bet you five bob that you smoke. Don't you?"

Elsie smiled, a smile which touched her eyes but yet did not take the very honest anxiety from them. She said:

"Well—yes, I do, sir."

"And don't you find," said Anthony, "that thinking's easier when you're smoking? . . . Course you do! Have one of these."

He slid off the table, held out his case, and, when she had taken a cigarette, lit a match for her. He said:

"You know, Elsie, that you told Superintendent Pike all that you could. Don't think I'm not

absolutely sure of that. What I'm trying to do is
to get you to try and remember *more* than you
remembered when you were talking to Superintendent Pike. After all—" his tone again was
most carefully blent. It had in it something of
the deliberately flattering appeal of man to
woman; something of the deliberate clarity of
adult explaining to child; something of essential friendliness; something of all these but not
too much of any—"after all, Elsie, you know as
well as I do, that when something has happened
which one hasn't taken much notice of, and then
afterward, when someone jumps up and tells
you that that thing which you didn't take much
notice of is very, very important, you get flus-
tered—at least I know I do—and then at the
time you say all that you remember quite truthfully, only to find afterward—perhaps it's a day,
perhaps it's even a week—that other things have
come back to you. You see what I mean?"

The girl was leaning forward in her chair
now, her gaze fixed on his face. She nodded.
"Yes, sir, I do. I know exactly."

"Right. Now then: all this business has been

a great shock to you, must have been. Therefore, it's quite probable, isn't it, that what you *think* is all you remember isn't *really* all you remember." He laughed a little here; a friendly laugh as if making mock of his own "funny way of talking." "You see what I mean, don't you? I'm not putting it very well, I'm afraid."

"Oh, yes, sir. I do indeed. What you mean is that sometime later, say perhaps next Sunday like, I shall sort of wake up and remember something that I didn't tell to the detective gentleman."

Anthony nodded. "Exactly, Elsie." Another smile; very friendly; perhaps a little more. "But what I want you to do now—I know it's difficult, and you may not be able to do it—but what I want you to *try* and do is to make that extra remembering—shall we call it?—come *now* instead of that next Sunday of yours. Understand me?"

"Yes, sir. Quite. But I don't see—" a worried frown had come between the brown eyes—"but I don't see—well, to tell you the truth, I don't see how to sort of start about it."

Anthony laughed. He said:

"You've nearly finished that cigarette. Throw it away and have another and I'll try and help you. I've done a bit of helping people like this before, Elsie. Some I've succeeded with, some I haven't. Let me try and help you."

The frown persisted but the mouth smiled. "Yes, sir," she said. But there was doubt in her tone.

Anthony kept great hold upon himself. It was essential that here he should seem to go slowly while really his mind was working faster perhaps than ever before. He said:

"Oh, it's not hypnotism or anything like that, Elsie. Don't look so frightened." More friendly still, this tone. A tone which held in it a teasing note. "Nothing like that about me, you know."

Elsie laughed, but a pink flush mounted to her cheeks. She said, as if against himself he had made some terrible allegation:

"Oh, no, sir. Of course not, sir."

Anthony cut her short. "All I meant, Elsie, was this: Instead of making you think and think and think and, if you know what I mean, just going round in circles inside your head, how would it be if I helped you to think the way I want you to think by asking you a few questions. You wouldn't mind that, would you?"

"Of course I shouldn't." Elsie's tone was both sharp and curt. "Don't you know I want to help?"

Anthony rejoiced both at the tone and the omission of the "sir"; it was the first sign that his efforts at making Elsie Polton into Elsie Polton instead of the pretty, well behaved parlourmaid who "was glad to say knew her place" were meeting with success. He said:

"That's right. Now you take this other cigarette I've been trying to offer you for the last few minutes . . . and this light . . . and then I'll take one and keep you company . . . and then we'll begin like this. . . . In a way, Elsie, this is like one of those games one plays at Christmas time. You know the sort of game where they send someone out of the room and he comes back and asks questions and you've only got to answer 'yes' or 'no.' You see what I'm driving at, don't you?"

Elsie nodded firmly. Now, definitely, she was Elsie Polton. She said crisply, in a tone quite different from any that had come from her before in this place: "Course I do. Go right on."

Anthony went right on. He said:

"You were in the dining room at Brooke Square at somewhere between five o'clock and half-past six, when you saw Miss Susan run down the steps?"

"Yes."

"Can you tell me—just forget anything you said to Superintendent Pike—can you give me any more exact time than this?"

"Yes." Elsie was entering whole-heartedly into this game; this game that meant so much.

"What time was it?"

"Can't say exactly, but it was nearer six than five and nearer half-past six than six."

"Right. Did you notice anything unusual about Miss Susan? Did she seem herself?"

"No. She seemed, well, very upset like."

"I see. She *ran* down the steps?"

"Yes."

"Did she turn left or right?"

"Left."

"Did she walk or run straight on after she had turned left. As if, I mean, she had got somewhere to go and knew where it was?"

"No. She seemed hesitating like. She was looking about the road. I thought perhaps she was looking for the captain's car."

"Then a taxi came along, didn't it?"

"Yes."

"Where was the taxi when you first saw it?"

"Just comin' round the corner out of Pool Street and turnin' down toward our house."

"And then it crossed over the road?—that is, onto its wrong side—onto the side that Miss Susan was walking along?"

"Yes."

"Did it just wander over, or did it cross over as if it was going to drop a fare at a house? Or did it——"

Elsie leant forward in her chair. Elsie raised a reproving finger. Elsie said:

"Now, not so many questions. Not all at once. Give me a chanst and I'll tell. . . . I'm remembering now—not but what I don't believe I told this to the detective gentleman. The taxi, when it swung out of Pool Street, well, it just made straight—sort of slantwise straight, if you know what I mean—straight at Miss Susan. And it stopped opposite her and she stopped as it stopped."

"I see. And what did she do then? Did the driver do anything?"

"No. Miss Susan looked in at the window. She seemed to be talking to somebody. She was waving her arm a bit. Seemed like as if she was very excited."

"And then?"

"And then she stopped wavin' her arm and sort of pulled open the door in a hurry like and jumped in. And then the taxi turned round."

"To its left, would that be?"

"Don't be silly. Of course he had to turn round left, otherwise he'd've gone over the pavement. . . . Well, anyway, the taxi turned round and was gone. I don't suppose I was watching more than a couple of minutes at the outside."

Anthony got up from the table. He began to walk about. He let Elsie cool for a moment. He said when he had judged that moment to have reached its judicious end:

"Now, Elsie. That's where, I think, you stopped with the superintendent. Is that so?"

Once more Elsie was almost the parlourmaid but not quite. She said: "Yes, sir. After all, sir, that's all I can remember. After I saw the taxi turn round, well, Miss Susan was gone, and there was nothing for me to watch and never is in that street. Nothink but page boys and cats, and I don't like neither."

Anthony came and stood before her, looking down upon her. When he spoke his voice was different; he was very grave and very deep. It impressed Elsie. "It went," said Elsie afterward to her friends, "sort of through a girl." He said:

"That, Elsie, is where you *think* you stop remembering. Now, it's up to us between us to find out whether there's not just something else that you remember."

"Yes, sir," said Elsie. Her dark eyes had now in them something of the pebbly glitter of the fascinated rabbit.

"You saw that taxi turn round, didn't you,

Elsie? I mean, you didn't go away from the window until after the taxi had turned round?"

"No, sir."

"So you saw the back of the taxi, Elsie?"

"Yes, sir."

"Now, Elsie, shut your eyes and think."

"Yes, sir." Elsie, obedient, closed her eyes.

"Elsie," Anthony's voice was very low and his words came slow. Each seemed to drop heavily into the silence left by its predecessor. "Think of what you saw of that taxi. What colour was it?"

Silence. And then:

"Red, sir. A sort of dirty red."

"Right. The top was shut?"

"Yes, sir."

"The top was shut. The taxi, or the back of it at least, was red. Was that back clean or dusty?"

Silence. And then:

"Dusty, sir. Sort of whity over the red, if you know what I mean." Still Elsie's eyes were closed. Her hands were clenched tightly in her lap; each cotton glove stretched almost to breaking point over a little fist.

"The taxi, when you saw the back of it, was red, had its top closed, and was dusty. . . . Now, keep those eyes shut, Elsie, and think. Think of that taxi. Make a picture of it inside your head. Red, dusty, tall. . . . Look at it going away from you; taking Miss Susan away from you! Look at it going toward Pool Street. Look at it, Elsie! Now, was there nothing else?"

The girl's eyes were now not merely closed but screwed up with the concentration of her effort. Anthony watched her. Sweat stood out in beads on his forehead. He leant forward, bending down over her. Even after he'd finished speaking his will went on fighting, trying to find points of contact with that other mind. Trying to force that other mind, points of contact or no points of contact, into submission.

Silence. Then a sigh. Then:

"No, sir. It's no good. I can't see anythink else." Very slow these words; very hopeless.

"Don't open your eyes. Think, girl, think! This isn't a party game. This is for Miss Susan. D'you know what may be happening to Miss Susan? D'you know that if we can't find Miss

Susan soon you may never see Miss Susan again?
D'you know that, Elsie? Think of that. . . .
Think. . . . Think of that taxi. *Make* your-
self think of it. *Now!*"

Silence.

The girl dropped her head into her hands;
rocked a little to and fro with the violence of her
effort.

Anthony watched her, his eyes blazing down
at her unseeing head.

And then, slowly, she began to speak. "No.
. . . it's no good. . . . OH! A bit of string.
. . . *A bit of string!*"

Silence. A silence which Anthony left as long
as he dared. He had to say at last:

"Yes. A bit of string? Where? On the taxi?"

"On the bottom of the back of the taxi." The
words were coming very slowly now as if each
were being drawn out by some process causing
bodily as well as mental pain. "A bit of string.
. . . Untidy. . . . Tied round something. . . ."

Silence again. Then, at last, Anthony's voice,
low, barely audible yet perfectly audible. Each
word a hard entity—each word like a bullet

nosing soft yet irresistible way into that other mind.

"That bit of string, Elsie. That bit of string. It's tying something on, isn't it?"

"Oh!" a shrill little squeal that word. The girl sits up. Her hands drop from her face. Her eyes open; stare widely open; there is a light in them. "Yes, yes! I can see it all now. How I came to forget, I don't know. It was his number plate. It was all sort of hanging loose on the skew-dab, if you know what I mean, sir, and he'd got it tied up with string and round and round. However I came to forget that I don't . . ."

But she found herself speaking to empty air. The door by which she had come in, the door of the room in which sat the captain and those other gentlemen, this door was open again. . . .

(3)

Into the heavy, taut silence of that other room Anthony entered like a gale. The three men at the moment of his entrance were seated, but he had barely crossed the threshold before all were on their feet.

"Got it!" he said. "Pike—forgive me, Lucas —put every damn man you've got onto this. A red taxi, top up, with a broken number plate tied up with string which brought a fare from farther west to Brooke Square and in Brooke Square picked up a lady at a quarter-past six this evening. Jump!"

Pike jumped. Heath's face was working. He said:

"What's this?"

"You sit down," said Anthony. "We're all right. We're onto something now. You wait."

"How long?"

Anthony was silent. "How long?" said Heath again, this time looking at Lucas. "Tell me!"

Lucas said, a little heavily:

"I'll be honest with you. It's something—it's a great deal. We can get that taxi. We might get it in an hour or we might get it in seven. Those are the limits."

Heath was silent. He turned his back to them

and walked away. He stared out of the window into the darkness. Lucas looked at Anthony.

"Gad, man! You look worn out! What you been doing? Third degree?"

Anthony mopped his face. "Third degree nothing! Svengali. What about a drink?"

"Alcoholic liquor," said Lucas, "is not allowed upon these premises." He went to the big cupboard in which were kept his outdoor clothes. From a drawer at its foot, which he unlocked with a key from his chain, he produced a bottle, a siphon and two glasses. "Say when," he said, and then, "Heath!"

Heath turned. "Have one?" said Lucas.

"Thanks!" Heath almost snatched at the glass, poured himself out a peg which came near to halfway, splashed into it a little soda, put the glass to his lips and drank. "Thank God!" he said, "for that! Look here, you fellows, is there a chance?"

"I don't know," said Anthony . . . "But I do know we're nearer something than we were twenty minutes ago. Here, let's have that glass, My subject wants one, I should think."

He took the glass and bottle and siphon, opened the door with two fingers, pushed it wide with his foot, went through it.

Elsie Polton was sitting where he had left her. Her eyes were closed, but at his approach they opened. She smiled at him; not quite the smile of the real Elsie Polton, but certainly not quite the smile of Elsie Polton, parlourmaid. He said:

"I'm a doctor, you know, and as a medical man I prescribe a little of this medicine for you. I expect—I don't know, but I expect—that you've tasted it before."

He poured out a drink, splashed soda into it, and gave her the glass. "It should be taken with tobacco." He opened his case and held it out.

"Thank you, sir," said Elsie simply. She took both glass and cigarette. She said, looking up at him:

"Don't know how it is, I feel real tired. Sort of as if all the strings had been pulled out of me, if you know what I mean." There were darker shadows under the dark eyes in a pale face.

"You drink that," Anthony said. "Back in a minute."

He was halfway to the door when she called him back. He heard her half-swallowed words and turned. She was standing up now, the cigarette dangling unheeded from her fingers, the glass in the other hand at such an angle that it was in danger of spilling its contents. She said:

"Could you tell me, sir—have I—is it—has there been any good like in what you made me remember?"

"Any good!" said Anthony. He came back toward her. He said: "You sit down again, my good child. You drink that and smoke that and see if you can't have a nap. It's comfortable there, isn't it? Any good! You'll see soon, Elsie. If we get to Miss Kerr, as I think we shall, it'll all be due to you."

He was gone. He was back once more in the inner room. Elsie stood a moment staring after him; then, as he had bidden her, went back to the chair.

Within the inner room, as Anthony entered, the telephone buzzed. Lucas was at it in one stride. Heath turned from the window. He stood tense; his face now was impassive, but with an impassiveness somehow shocking.

"Yes?" said Lucas. "Yes. . . . Yes. . . . You've what? . . . You *haven't!* . . . Good God! All right. . . . Yes, yes, take *all* the cars if you want 'em. . . . Hurry, man. Hurry! . . ."

He put down the receiver on its hook. He got up slowly. Still his eyes were astonished. He said very quietly:

"That was Pike. They've found that taxi already!"

"Hallelujah!" said Anthony.

Heath took half a step forward; opened his mouth. He seemed about to say something, but there came from him only a little strangled noise, dead as soon as it was born.

"Yes," said Lucas. He looked at Heath. "Luck's beginning to be with us now. That's the quickest find I've ever known in years. It's a Kensington taxi, in Baron's Garage. The driver's off duty, but they've got his address. Pike's going round there now." He looked at his watch. "Let's see, the streets are clear, Ross is driving. . . . They'll get there in seven minutes. They ought to be back here nearly within twenty."

They were, in fact, within twenty-two. Pike and a short, fat, untidy, and bewildered being whose name, it appeared, was incongruously Periwinkle. Mr. Periwinkle, having been dragged from an early bed, was not only frightened but cross. But Mr. Periwinkle was handled —handled firmly and yet kindly. It was Anthony who gave him a drink. After that drink Mr. Periwinkle's seeming reluctance to part with information became miraculously changed to an almost scout-like desire to help.

Mr. Periwinkle put down the glass with a little smack upon Lucas's mantelpiece. "Ar, yerss!" said Mr. Periwinkle. "Corst I remembers. I'm a man as never fergits not nothink. Wonderful mem'ry I've got! Yerss! These fares you're talkin' about, the first one, 'e picks me up round the back of Queen's Club there. 'E sez, 'Got a long job fer you, cabby.' I sez, 'Yerss, hop in.' An' 'e 'opped in. Told me to drive direck to Jook Square: when I gets there 'e'd di-

reck me again. Just as we turns the corner into
Jook Square from Pool Street, 'e 'ollers down
my speakin'-choob—an' I'd 'ave you know, gentlemen, as my speakin'-choob is a speakin'-choob
that you *can* speak froo. It's not just a lump o'
rubber wiv a nozzle on the end to misguide
folks. It's a speakin'-choob!—Well, my fare, 'e
'ollers down the speakin'-choob so stutterin'
loud 'e nearly wrecks my eardrum. 'E sez: 'See
that lady just come out of that 'ouse? I want to
pick 'er up.' So I slews across, sir, an' we picks
up a little piece, sir—a very smart young lady
wot 'ad just come out of one of the 'ouses. I think
it was number firteen."

"Half a minute, Periwinkle." This from
Lucas. "Did the lady seem to be expecting a car
or taxi?"

"Oh, yerss! At least, it looked that way to me.
Not as I was takin' much notice like, me bein' a
man as just does his job and takes no notice of
nuffink. But, yerss, now you come to mention it,
it did seem as if the lady was expectin' some-
think. But, anyways, I drove up alongside of
'er, on the right-'and side that is, that's my

wrong side, if you foller me, sir, accordin' to the instructions down my choob. Then the lady, she looks in at my fare froo the winder and she lets out some sort of a little squeak. Well, I thinks, that's a bit funny, but I starts to turn round, and then I thinks, 'Well, t'ain't none o' Bert Periwinkle's business, and that's that.' I just sits there, and as long as the clock's tickin' I'm 'appy."

"But where did you go, man?" Heath had come forward now. His hands were clenched into fists, his whole body stiff. He seemed poised on his toes as if for some instant action.

"Shut up, blast you!" said Anthony into his ear, so savagely that even through his anguish the man heard, and not only heard but appreciated. He muttered in his throat and fell back again out of the little group into the shadows from which he had come.

Mr. Periwinkle rolled a watery eye in the interrupter's direction.

"Comin' to that," said Mr. Periwinkle, "in joo course. I tells the story in me own way or not at all, an' I'm not frightened of no man, bein' honest meself. Not even if I *am* in Scotland Yard!"

"Now, then, Periwinkle, cut all that out!" Pike's voice, crisp and official. Then, in the man's ear, Anthony's whisper:

"Ten bob if you keep your shirt in, Periwinkle. Stick it!"

Periwinkle stuck it. He picked upon Lucas to talk to. He said:

"Shall I go on, sir, or do I jest answer questions like?"

"Go on! Go on!" said Lucas. "Did the lady get in?"

"Yerss, sir, just what I was a-comin' to before all these interruptions. An' we should 'a' bin there a sight quicker if it 'adn't bin for all these interruptions. . . ."

"Go on, man. Go on!"

"Well, the lady gets in, sir, seeming to 'ave recovered from that little sort of shock like that made 'er give that little squeak I told you about just now. And then my fare—the bloke—'e picks up the choob again and yells froo it, 'Victoria.' "

A gasp—Heath's—from the background.

"Yerss," said Mr. Periwinkle. "Victoria, 'e shouts, and nearly splits me yeerole agen. The fact is, it's still buzzin'." He put a tentative finger into his left ear, probed gently with a gentle look of inquiry upon his face, shook his head, and resumed.

"So to Victoria I goes, sir. And at Victoria out gets my fares, and the bloke pays me, and off I goes, and that's all, sir, as I c'n tell you, thankin' you kindly for the same!"

Pike cut in: "Now, Periwinkle, did you get a look at your fares at all?"

"Oh, yerss! I've told you wot the young lady looked like, and anyway you all seems to know, as it's 'er you're bothered about."

"That's enough, Periwinkle! What was the man like?"

"Tallish," said Mr. Periwinkle. "Stiffish build; toff. 'Drave me lake L to Jook Squaw.' Genuine, I'd say. None of your Palay de Darns stuff."

"Clean shaven?" It was Anthony's turn.

"Oh, yerss!"

"Whereabouts at Victoria did you drop them? Station yard?" Pike.

"I said Victoria and I meant Victoria. W'ere else at Victoria would you drop a fare that arst to go to Victoria except the station yard? Yerss, station yard, it was."

"You see where they went? In which direction?" Lucas.

"So far as I can rec'leck, sir—" Mr. Periwinkle obviously knew his world. He, if not Elsie Polton, knew the difference between his commissioner and his superintendent of police—"so far as I can rec'leck, sir," said Mr. Periwinkle again, "into the station they did go. Under the canopy and down what you might call the first alleyway."

"What time did they get to Victoria?" Anthony.

"As near as I can say, sir—" Mr. Periwinkle did not know who this other tall gentleman might be, but he kept upon the safe side—"as near as I can say, sir, somewhere around fifteen minutes of seven."

"I see." This from Lucas. "Pike, this man can go. Got that car downstairs?"

"Yes, sir."

"Got any men by it?"

"Three, sir."

"Right." Lucas looked at Anthony. "Victoria, I think, don't you, Gethryn?"

Anthony nodded. He had his wallet in his hand. From it he had abstracted a ten-shilling note which, cosily folded, found its way a moment later into Mr. Periwinkle's receptive hand.

(4)

Once more the blue police car and the black Voisin-Maxwell were parked tail to nose. They were in the fore court of Victoria Station. By them were four men: the driver of the police car and three plain-clothes detectives. At the other side of the station, in an austere, barely furnished, and cleanly room which yet smelt of a thousand engines, were Lucas and Pike, Heath and Anthony. They sat stiffly upon stiff wooden chairs, rigidly arranged to face the station master's table. Behind that table was the station master himself, slightly pompous, very kindly, genuinely perturbed, and entirely efficient. To the right of the table stood, not at all at ease, the third of the ticket collectors who had appeared before this conclave.

"Very well, Briggs," said the station master. "You can go. Tell the next man to come in."

Heath, sitting beside Anthony, shifted uneasily.

"Wait," said Anthony.

The fourth man came in. Younger than his predecessors, pleasanter to the eye, more self-assertive.

"Travers," said the station master, "you were on number six gate on second shift?"

"Yes, sir." Travers's voice was as smart as his appearance.

"I think you are an observant man, Travers. Now, you must have passed in on your shift hundreds of young couples of whom the man was dark and tall and the young woman short and fair?"

"Thousands, more like, sir."

"Exactly. Now these gentlemen, Travers, are from Scotland Yard."

"Yes, sir," said Travers. He strived, not very successfully, to keep his eye from dwelling on the sleuths.

"They want, Travers, to trace the destination of a tall, dark, clean-shaven, well dressed young man, probably giving first-class tickets, who had with him a short, fair, smartly dressed and very charming young lady."

"Yes, sir."

"*Very* smartly dressed," Anthony put in quietly. "*Very* charming."

"Think of that, Travers."

"Yes, sir," said Travers.

"These gentlemen think," said the station master, "that it is possible that the young lady was appearing ill. That's their theory, you see. . . . Yes, Travers, you can speak if you like."

"Seen 'em, sir," said Travers. His tone was even crisper, his words even quicker than before. Under his trim exterior he plainly seethed with the excitement of the chase and the prominent part which he himself might play in it.

"When did you see this couple, Travers?"
The station master's voice again. "Don't answer
too quickly. Think before you speak."

"Yes, sir." It was plain that Travers knew;
equally plain that he was obeying instructions
and thinking, albeit quite unnecessarily, before
he spoke. "Yes, sir. . . . They went by the
seven fifty-three Marsham–Hailsbury fast, sir."

The station master held up a finger for silence. He looked at Lucas. "Now, sir, I think
perhaps we have found our man. Perhaps you
would like to take on the questioning of this collector? Travers, just answer as briefly as you can
all the questions this gentleman likes to put to
you."

"Yes, sir."

"Travers," said Lucas, "give us your description of this couple you think are the people
we're looking for."

"Yes, sir. Tall gentleman, very well dressed,
sort of half-country, half-London clothes.
Tweeds, if you know what I mean, sir. Age anywhere between thirty and forty, sir. Dark com-
plexion, clean-shaven, heavy build, full face,

sir. Young lady, much younger, very small, sir, *very* pretty like. Young lady didn't seem to be well, sir. Gentleman had his arm round her. Her eyes were half closed. She didn't seem to know where she was, like. While I was clipping the tickets, sir, the gentleman kept saying, 'It's all right. It's all right. You'll be all right as soon as I can get you sitting down in the train.' The gentleman apologized for holding the tickets awkward. Said the lady had been taken queer but would be all right in a minute."

Lucas bent forward in his chair. Even into his practised official monotone there crept an easily discernible anxiety. "Travers," he said slowly, "you don't, I suppose, happen to remember the destination on the tickets that this man gave you?"

Travers smiled; a brief smile, eminently respectful, of self-esteem. "Oh, yes, but I do, sir!"

"What?" Lucas, startled out of his calm, half rose from his chair.

"I remember quite well, sir. Owing to the way he was standing, holding the young lady and all, the gentleman dropped the tickets. I bent down and picked them up. That's what fixed the destination in my mind. The tickets were for Chasing Bury."

"Where's that?"

The station master answered this one. "It's a small station about forty miles down the line between Horfield and Clissop."

Heath half rose from his chair, but Anthony's hand forced him down again. Lucas was saying:

"Does that train stop at this place?"

"Yes, sir," said Travers before the station master could speak. "After Horfield it stops at Chasing Bury, Little Benders, and Ockleton. Then there's no stop till Marsham itself."

Lucas rose. He said to the station master:

"We're much obliged, sir. What's the next train?"

"To Chasing Bury?" The station master thought a moment. "Let me see, is there one?"

"Excuse me, sir." The self-complacent Travers once more. "Excuse me, sir, if these gentlemen was to move, sir, they could catch the eleven twenty-one and change at Bramingham Junction. There'll be a wait there of ten minutes, and they could catch the branch mail to Chasing Bury."

The gentlemen moved.

(5)

But they did not go down to Chasing Bury by rail. Upon a table in the long room of the Victoria refreshment bar they spread maps; pored over them; found their route.

The police car was the first to start. But the police car only held its lead for some two hundred yards down the Vauxhall Bridge Road. Then the Voisin-Maxwell drew abreast. From the seat beside the driver Heath leaned out and shouted. The police car pulled up. From the offside window was thrust Lucas's head. Anthony called:

"Lucas! Let me have a policeman?"

The head nodded; was withdrawn. The door upon the far side of the saloon opened and shut, and presently, with them, climbing into the back seat, was a smiling Pike. The two cars moved off. Once more Lucas leaned out of the window. This time he shouted:

"You may be there first. If you get anything, leave word at the station."

Anthony raised his left hand in salute and acknowledgment; and then his left hand came down to the wheel again. The big car shot forward. In the back seat Pike gasped. In the seat beside the driver's Heath leant forward, crouching. His feet were pressed hard against their sloping support. He was, with all his will, urging the great car forward. The faster it went, the faster he wished it would go. No pace that night would have been too much for Heath. . . .

The driver of the police car—the best and at the same time the most notoriously speed-thirsty driver in the police force—did his best. But when all is said and done, a driver's best is his car's; and the police car's best is seventy miles an hour. After that salute of Anthony's the others did not see, upon that forty-mile run down the Portsmouth Road, even so much as the flicker of his tail light. It was not a journey that Pike cares to remember. He is, when asked about it, very reticent. Heath remembers nothing because he was noting nothing. Heath, for

this time, was an Idea. None of the three spoke
on that drive until it was within four miles of
its end. The great lights showed suddenly a
crossroad. In the centre a green hillock had,
sticking up out of it like a finger, a signpost.
Anthony pulled the big car to a standstill. He
switched on his spotlight.

Pike stood up in the back seat. "Right-hand
fork, sir," he said. "Chasing Bury, three miles."

Heath twisted in his seat, his first movement
since the beginning of that rush through the
night. He muttered something which they
couldn't catch and was silent again.

The car started, swung slowly right; gathered
speed.

They were driving down a narrow, not ill-
surfaced Surrey lane. Upon either side of them
were green banks. Along the tops of the banks
were great trees whose green arms met above
their heads. A tunnel of green and black; a tunnel whose floor turned into a blazing river
under the car's lights. . . .

And at the other end of the tunnel their destination.

The clock upon Anthony's speedometer stood at ten minutes past twelve. Over his shoulder Anthony spoke to Pike:

"Station first, I think."

"Yes, sir."

They found it easily enough, for they came, after passing the straggling outskirts of the village, down a hill and under a railway bridge. The station stood at the top of the hill upon the bridge's other side. It was in darkness. It was locked. They stood upon the pavement and looked about them. Anthony went back to the car; swivelled his spotlight; shone its beam this way and that.

"There!" said Heath. "There! Isn't that a cottage?"

"That's it, sir." Beside him Pike ran. Together they followed the white palings leading to the station master's garden. Anthony stayed by the car. Pike found a door, beat upon it with the knocker. No answer.

Heath shouldered him aside; took the knocker and wrought with it. . . .

Success. Above their heads a window was

thrown open. From above their heads came a
stream of abuse at their night-rending practice.
Pike, nudging Heath, stated who he was and
why. Within two and a half minutes he and
Heath were standing just within the passage of
the station master's cottage. The station master,
an old overcoat over his nightshirt, his feet
tucked into wool-lined slippers several sizes too
small for him, strove to atone. Yes, it *was* part
of his duty to collect tickets for the night
trains. . . . Yes, he did start these duties before eight. . . . Yes, he had done so to-night.
. . . Yes, he did, now the gentleman came to ask
him, think he remembered a strange lady and
gentleman getting off the eight-forty. But then
there was quite a crowd on that train always,
and it was a bit hard, with only one's self to
take the tickets and all, to remember. One didn't
seem to have much time for looking at faces.

Heath seized his arm and shook it. "You *must*
have seen the man! You must! Tell me!"

Pike soothed the ruffled third. "It's this gentleman whose wife has been abducted. Stolen
away, you might call it."

The station master clicked a sympathetic tongue.

"So you see," said Pike, "how very important it is that you try and remember."

The station master strove. He seemed unable to think without grunting. Judging by the man and the number of his grunts, he now was thinking hard and harder. He spoke at last, just as they had despaired of hearing his voice again. He said, with a ponderous slowness:

"Would the party you was looking for be a stout, elderly man and a stoutish lady not quite so old?"

There came a muttered oath from Heath; the flinging open of the door; the banging of the door. He was gone.

"Tck-tck!" said the station master.

Pike saw by the light of the single candle that the grizzled head was being shaken slowly from side to side. A voice came from the head even as it was moving. "That'd be all. Except of course, a young leddy and gennlemun, but they wouldn't be——"

"Young lady and gentleman? What sort of young lady and gentleman?"

"First class. Straight from Lunnon. Tallish, stiffish-built, youngish gentleman; smallish leddy." The station master cackled suddenly. "If that's them you're lookin' for, I think him that's just gone out had best save himself. Very lovin' an' all this lot were. Had his arm round her. An' on the public platform! *And* she was leanin' 'gainst him! Where's your 'duction there? Eh?"

"You didn't," said Pike, "notice where they went, I suppose? Which way?"

The head was shaken again. "Couldn't tell you nought. They took one o' Stevens's cabs."

"Where does *he* live?" Pike's tone was growing curt. "Stevens, I mean?"

"Stevens? Would it be Joe or young Jim you be meanin'?"

"The one," said Pike, "that runs the cabs."

"Ah! That's Charlie. Charlie, he lives over t'other side of the yard. Over yonder. Over his mother's 'baccy shop. But if you think that Charlie Stevens—— Hi, mister!"

But now the station master stood alone. His front door was open, and a chill night breeze played about his bony ancient ankles. He muttered. He shut the door, muttering still. He went up to bed and to sleep. He waked in the morning, uncertain as to whether the whole affair had been dream or reality. . . .

(6)

Now there were two cars in the station yard at Chasing Bury. The police car had caught up. Over the road, outside the newspaper shop which bore over its single window the name L. WIDDIMAN, stood a little group of five. Inside the room, immediately above the Widdiman window, were Pike and Anthony. They were talking to Mr. Charles Stevens who "ran the cabs."

Mr. Charles Stevens was a red-faced and burly man. He was also, though his looks belied him, a man of ready intelligence. Mr. Charles Stevens grasped, as quickly as it was said, the whole meed. Also he was helpful. He said:

"No trouble at all, gentlemen. I 'aven't got to

think, becos I drove the pair meself. Can't be mistaken, 'cause they were strangers!"

"You can't tell us where the house is?" said Pike. "Where they went?"

"It's a sure thing I can, mister. It's that new two-storied cottage Cockerinn put up last year. 'Bout three or four mile out along the Harling road."

Mr. Stevens was thanked quickly. Mr. Stevens was left even more quickly. With the slamming of the door the group upon the pavement sprang to life. Pike spoke hurriedly with Lucas; with the driver of the police car. The party split as before. By the signpost at the corner of the station yard they saw that Harling lay four miles to the east.

The police car was off first. But once more the Voisin-Maxwell in two hundred yards passed it with a roaring boom.

(7)

"Good!" said Anthony. "Follow along, will you?"

They were working—he and Pike and Heath

—round to the back of the two-storied cottage called—for once appropriately—"The Firs." They were in a copse of firs. They had struck off from the road a hundred yards before the cottage. In front, at the other side of the house, were Lucas and the others.

Anthony led the way out of the firs, crossed a small paddock of rough pasture, wriggled through a wire fence, and was in the cottage garden. . . .

In one of the four ground-floor windows of the cottage a light was burning. Anthony halted; then went on again. Pike now drew level. Behind them, admirably, kept Heath. They crossed a small lawn. On the dew-drenched grass they moved without sound. The lawn came to an abrupt end, and they were on a small flagged walk which separated for the whole of its length the house from the grass. The pink glow from behind the curtained French window to their left still shone softly. Toward this window, moving now upon tiptoe, they went in single file.

It was as Anthony set careful fingers to the

window latch that, from the other side of the house, came the sound of knocking. To Pike at his elbow Anthony whispered approval. The knocking ceased, but only for a moment; it began again with redoubled clamour. A thunderous noise.

Pike pressed his ear to the window; suddenly stiffened; suddenly held up a finger for silence.

The knocking went on. The three outside the window held their breath. Against his shoulder Anthony could feel Heath's fingers pressing, digging into the flesh. Pike whispered:

"Somebody's just gone out of this room."

The knocking ceased. The silence which followed it was broken by the rattle of chain and bolt.

"Now!" said Anthony. Together he and Pike threw their shoulders against the centre struts of the window frame. With a little tearing, rending noise it gave. Pike staggered, caught his foot on the inch-high sill, and fell headlong into the room. After him Anthony reeled; with a wrench recovered himself. As he stood, now

firmly upright, something brushed violently past him—Heath.

But the room was otherwise empty. Anthony's eyes, in one swift circular glance, took in this room and its furnishings. A small room but pleasant, with trappings and fitments pleasing enough in their way.

Heath was at the door now. Suddenly, with a wrench, he had it open. . . .

From the floor Pike picked himself up; was on Anthony's heels at the door through which Heath had just now gone. Just across the threshold Anthony checked. Into his back, unable to stop, Pike crashed. "Sorry, sir!" he grunted. "Now, where the *Jing* . . . !"

"Ssh . . . !" Anthony's warning was savage. "Listen!"

They listened. They were standing at one end of a long and narrow hall. At the other end was the front door, and the front door was open. And from just inside it there came a voice. Lucas's. Anthony's fingers groped the wall opposite him; pressed the switch. Light flooded the place. The first thing that these two saw was

Heath. He stood three feet in front of them. He was motionless, but his body was bent forward from the hips. His arms were crooked, their hands reaching out a little way before him. He looked like an animal checked in mid-spring; an animal checked by astonishment.

Past him they looked now, to see the cause of that astonishment. At the other end of the hall, just within the half-open door, Lucas stood facing them. But Lucas had not seen them. Lucas's head and gaze were downbent as he talked to someone—a woman, with her back to them. A small, slight figure—very neat. Under the lamp the head glinted with a sheen of coppery gold.

It seemed to Anthony as if neither he nor any of this group moved for quite an appreciable time. They were, he thought, like a suddenly arrested moving picture. It seemed to him, as indeed it must have seemed to them all, incredible that here was Susan, and a Susan—even just by that one glimpse of her back—utterly unfrightened, quite unhurt, completely and happily herself. . . .

For another long wavering moment the tableau seemed to hold. Then by Heath it was shattered. It was as if an image in a pool had been broken by the plumping of a rock.

Heath moved. From his throat there came a cry, half groan, half exultation. In a flash the little figure at the far end of the passage whipped round.

"Trevor!" she said. Her arms came out; she took half a step forward, but not more than half a step. Before that half step could be a whole one Heath was upon her.

Past these two, interlocked and oblivious, Lucas picked delicate way. Pike and Anthony came to meet him. They stood, the three of them, silent. Lucas spoke first.

"If somebody," he said, "will tell me that I'm still awake I'd be obliged."

Pike scratched his head He said:

"Well, it won't be me, sir I can't get the feel of this!"

Anthony grinned. "You know what's the matter with you, police, is that you're disappointed. You came rushing through the night hoping to find dismembered parts of the lady packed away behind the bath, and when you do find her, she's all in one and apparently not needing your efforts at all. And you just can't bear it!"

But Pike was taking no chaff. He was too puzzled. He repeated: "I can't get the *feel* of this, sir! I haven't spoken to her, but I'll take my oath that young lady's not even worried!"

"She isn't," said Lucas. He stood a moment, then turned on his heel; walked back purposefully to the lovers. Pike followed. Anthony, content with the onlooker's part, sat down upon a table and began to feel for his cigarette case. He heard Lucas's voice.

"Miss Kerr," it was saying. "Miss Kerr, I'm sorry, but I must ask you to give me your attention. . . ."

Anthony's smile widened into a grin.

"Course she will, Lucas! Course she will!" This was Heath, but this, thought Anthony, was the real Heath. This was a Heath with a different voice, a Heath who seemed fifteen years younger and a stone or two heavier than the man who had been with them throughout the night. Heath and Susan stood now, arm locked in arm. The top of Susan's golden poll was not quite level with her lover's shoulder.

Lucas was saying: "How did you get here? *Why* did you get here? If it comes to that, Miss Kerr, *who* brought you here? ¡Was it Trenchard?"

Susan nodded brightly. "Yes, poor man. He's very, very tired. He's upstairs, sleeping. Think how tired he must have been when your knocking didn't wake him up."

Lucas put a hand to his forehead in bewilderment. Heath stiffened. For a moment there came a return to his face of that pinched and bleak and ravaged seeming. Susan looked up, laid a hand on his arm.

"Trevor!" she said. That was all. But it was enough.

"But   Trenchard . . . Trenchard . . . He . . . Did you come . . . How did he . . ." Lucas was battling bravely with his reeling mind.

Anthony, through the smoke of his cigarette, looked at Lucas's face and then at Pike's. And if Lucas's face made him smile, Pike's made him put his head back and laugh aloud. That laugh seemed to be the quick-match for Lucas's temper. He turned; he glared. He took two steps forward and said:

"Yes, you can laugh, Gethryn! But if you're so blasted clever, perhaps *you'll* explain to-night for me."

Anthony got to his feet. "My dear fellow, I wouldn't even try. I'm just as much at sea as you are. But I'm not a disappointed policeman! I'm merely a pleased civilian. You wait, my lad, you'll hear!"

He looked over toward the lovers. "Miss Kerr will tell you." He raised his voice. "Miss Kerr!"

She looked up questioningly.

Anthony, still smiling, went toward her. "Miss Kerr," he said again, "I wonder whether you realize what a shock you've given us?" He looked at her. "Yes, I expect you do. I'd like to suggest that we find somewhere in this house to sit down and then hear from you exactly how you come to be here. What, in other words, the whole business is about."

"I think," said a voice—a new voice from behind and above them—"I think that ought to be my job."

Five pairs of eyes went to the stairhead. In the third stair, coming down toward them, was Trenchard. He was dressed still in the "tweedy clothes" described by the ticket collector Travers at Victoria Station, but they were no longer very smart seeming. They were, in fact, rucked and rumpled and creased, and his black hair—wiry, kinky black hair—stood up now in wild disorder. There was about the whole man the appearance of one just roused from sleep. He blinked at the light. His heavy face was dead white. He looked first at Susan and then from Susan to the four men. There was in that look a certain sort of apologetic defiance.

For an appreciable moment nobody moved; no one spoke. Anthony was silent from choice, the other men because—although a moment ago they had thought they would, when see Trenchard they did, have plenty to say—they found themselves now without a word. When you have been rushing over a quarter of England in search of a man who has, most blackguardly, stolen away a young woman, and then you find the young woman is no more perturbed than was Susan Kerr, your mind, to whatever class it belongs, cries out for readjustment. It was Anthony who broke the silence. He looked at Trenchard and said:

"I was suggesting to Miss Kerr, as you heard, that we find somewhere to sit down and hear all about it. This your house?"

Trenchard nodded; a wry, rather bitter smile crossed for a moment his heavy white face. "Yes," he said. He pushed through the little group. He threw open a door. After him the party filed. They stood in a small dining room. Round the oak table Trenchard set chairs. "If you'd all sit down," he said.

They sat down. Lucas found his voice. Lucas said:

"I think it only fair to tell you, sir, that I'm not yet certain whether a charge lies against you or not. If we find eventually that it does, then anything you tell us now——"

"I know! I know!" said Trenchard, " 'may

be taken down and used as evidence against me.'
That doesn't matter, and I rather fancy, you
know, that there won't be a charge." He looked
at Susan. "Miss Kerr," he said, "has already
told me that she won't charge me, and I don't
see that anyone else can in these circumstances.
The worst I've been is a damn fool."

He stood at the end of the table, looking
round upon the seated five. There was a chair
beside him, but he did not sit. He rested his
hands upon the table. He said, in a flat, heavy
voice like that of a man exhausted:

"Just damn' foolishness, that's all it's been.
. . . I take it you want the truth without em-
broideries and in as few words as possible?"

Lucas nodded and Pike said: "Certainly."

Trenchard looked down at the table. He
spoke still in that tired voice, only lower now,
almost as if he were speaking to himself. He
said:

"From the time she was sixteen, until she—
died—I was in love—very much in love—with
Eve. When she was eighteen I began asking her
to marry me. For a time it looked as if she

would. I had to wait because her parents thought she wasn't old enough to decide. That waiting—did me in. Three years ago she met Hale-Storford. He fell in love with her and she with him. They married within eighteen months. I never met Hale-Storford before they were married—I didn't want to. I was away when the engagement was announced, and I stayed away. Then I went down—not knowing, mind you, anything about Hale-Storford having taken the house in the neighbourhood—to stay with old Banner in Wessex. We went out for a sail, as we always did, one evening and got driven ashore just below Hale-Storford's house. He saw us and came down and was very decent, I must say. We went in, stayed to dinner, and stayed the night. . . ."

Here Trenchard at last raised his head. He looked once more round at the seated party; looked, in fact, at each in turn, but each pair of eyes that met his were meeting, and knew they were meeting, eyes which did not really see them. Trenchard moistened dry lips with his tongue. He went on. He was now speaking more slowly, it was as if each word and the production of each word were an effort to him. He said:

"I can tell you, I got a pretty nasty jolt when I found whose house I was in. There was Eve, looking more beautiful, I think, than ever I'd seen her before. She was, as always, delightful to me. I kept telling myself that she must be happy, but somehow, I can't tell you when or how, something seemed to me to be wrong. . . . Perhaps that was only a premonition. I don't know much about those things. Can't say I've ever believed in them before. Anyhow, I'm not going to tell you the rest of what happened that night. You know for yourselves, all of you. I can only say—" very slowly his words were coming now; he seemed to stumble over some of them—"I can only say," he repeated, "that when Hale-Storford and Banner and I went upstairs and found—and found what you know we found, I thought for the rest of that night that I was going to lose my reason. . . ."

He stopped. He squared his shoulders, put back his head, and gave a little sound which was meant, it seemed, to be a laugh. A most distressing sound.

"But I didn't!" he said. "Not on your life I didn't. Nothing so pleasant as *that* happened to me. I just went on being sane and suffering and hoping against hope that they'd find out whichever devil had done that—that—whichever devil it was and hang him. Or her. Though hanging, I thought, was a damn sight too good. . . ."

He put out a hand behind him and groped with it; found the chair, pulled it toward him, and sat heavily and quickly—almost as if his legs had on a sudden betrayed him. "That's all," he said, and now his voice had in it so queer a deadness that the eyes of Susan came round to him, big with pity. "All, I mean, that it's necessary to say to lead up to to-night. What happened to me was this: I *knew* that either that woman Graye, that boy Anstruther, or her sister, had killed Eve. *Knew* it, I tell you! Knew it because as I was down there all that time with Hale-Storford himself and Banner—neither of them could have done it—and no one, whatever the puling fools at the inquest said, could have got into that house and done it and got out again without being found out."

Across the table Pike's small and now very bright brown eyes sought Anthony's. Anthony nodded.

". . . knew it, I tell you!" Trenchard was saying. His fist banged down on the table. A glass bowl which stood in centre of the table rang softly. "Knew it! And I had to sit there day after day after damnable day, watching whichever devil it was get away with it. And then—you all know this—the Rossiter woman ran her car over that cliff and was blotted out. And then the Anstruther boy was drowned. Those were supposed to be *accidents*."

Again across the table Pike and Anthony exchanged a glance.

"But," said Trenchard, "I couldn't see them as accidents. I *wouldn't* see them as accidents! Four people, and one of them guilty of the foulest crime, and two of them suddenly to die *accidentally!* I didn't believe, and by God!"—again his fist hit the table—"I don't believe it now!

. . . What I believed—what I *believe,* is that
the devil who killed Eve turned into a frightened devil; thought that—perhaps going a little
mad—one of the four must have seen or heard
something dangerous which at sometime would
come out. . . ."

He looked round the room again at his audi-
ence, this time with eyes which saw them, and
in his eyes—dark eyes with a fire behind their
darkness—was something of appeal.

"Don't you see," he said, "don't you see that
I'm right? You must! You're not fools like those
damn country bobbies and that doddering coroner! You must see! I'm not mad, I know that!
Sometimes I wish to God I were! . . . Four
people, one guilty, and two of them gone. Who
were the two that were left? The woman Graye
and—and Miss Kerr. Now, I haven't been down
in Wessex all the time. I left as soon as I could,
but I've kept abreast of Polferry news through
Banner, and I knew, or thought I knew, the
woman Graye hadn't been in a position to cause
these accidents. Who then was left? Miss Kerr."
Across the dead white pallor of his face an

ironic smile of self-derision flashed momentarily. "I didn't, you see, know Miss Kerr so well as I do now. I thought—perhaps I didn't reason enough, but I thought it *must* be Miss Kerr, and I thought—damn it, I almost knew! —that the police were doing nothing. Was I to watch what I thought was the devil who killed Eve make itself safe by killing all those who might possibly be dangerous to it? I couldn't. I tried to stick it out; I even went away; but I couldn't. I kept coming back to—to——"

He suddenly put his elbows on the table and into his cupped hands dropped his forehead, but his voice went on. "I saw her, you know. Eve, I mean. None of *you* did! P'r'aps if you had you would—— Well, that's no matter. I've done what I've done. I began to look out for a chance to get Miss Kerr, thinking that she was the devil I was looking for, where I could make her—" words now were coming through barely opening lips—"make her," he repeated, "confess. I took to watching her. I think I was good at it. And I found that she was always with you." He said these words straight at Heath.

"And I had to get rid of you, so I did that hospital story. I sent you off to that hospital for Miss Kerr, and I got Miss Kerr away by the same dodge about you. I came in that taxi. I told her I was from the hospital. When she saw me, of course, she knew who I was. But I told her some damn lie, and got her into the cab."

"It was a very good lie," said Susan.

"Once I'd got her in the cab, I——" He seemed to choke. He raised his head; he said slowly: "I drugged her—I'll give you all details of that afterward if you want to take me—and got her down here by train, pretending she was ill. I brought her into this room; waited until she came round. . . . When she came round I began to talk to her. I told her what I've told you, only more. I told her——"

Susan's voice interrupted; said very clearly and very kindly:

"Mr. Trenchard, I don't think it's necessary, you know, to tell too much. I've forgotten, you see. So . . ."

Trenchard smiled at her, a real smile this time which lit quite magically the saturnine mask of his heavy face. He said, looking now at Lucas:

"You hear that, sir? That's the sort of woman Miss Kerr is. I've told you I'm not mad, and so it didn't take me long to find out that I'd made a mistake, and a ghastly mistake. You see, I didn't know Miss Kerr well—not at all, in fact. We had been together in the house at Polferry, we had been together a little during those weeks of the inquest, but we had never known each other. If we had, I'd never have made—never have been such a fool. . . . After Miss Kerr had talked to me, I saw . . .

"That's all, I think." His big body slumped as he sat. He seemed, suddenly, to have lost all force. He sat staring straight across the table at Lucas.

Silence, heavy and acutely discomfortable.

"Miss Kerr," said Lucas. His voice was tersely and monotonously official. "Have you any charge to make against this man?"

Susan smiled, a smile which robbed the words which came after it of much of their sting. "Isn't that rather silly?" said Susan. "I should have thought you'd have gathered that by this time."

"In that case," said Lucas, looking now at Pike, "the matter for the time, at least, stays where it is. Miss Kerr, if you'd like to get back to London we can take you in the police car."

"I say," said Anthony mildly, "if nobody minds, I think I'd like to ask Mr. Trenchard a question or so."

Trenchard lifted his heavy head; nodded it.

"I'd like to ask," said Anthony, "whether, Trenchard, you've given up your idea that it was one of those four who killed Mrs. Hale-Storford."

Trenchard stiffened. "No!" he said, and then again, "No!"

"Meaning . . . ?" said Anthony.

"Graye," said Trenchard. Once more he was erect in his chair. Once more his eyes had that fire behind their darkness.

Anthony looked at him. "If," he said, "I were to tell you, or rather get Superintendent Pike here to tell you, that it's quite impossible—and I'm using the word in its real and fullest sense

—for Mrs. Graye to have been the author of these *accidents,* what would you say?"

Trenchard looked at him for a long moment before speaking.

"I don't," he said, "know who you are, but you look as if you're talking the truth as you know it. What I'd say is that perhaps after all I'm wrong in thinking myself sane."

Anthony leaned his arms upon the table. He gazed steadily at Trenchard. They looked at each other, these two. It was as if, almost, they were alone. Anthony said:

"And what would you say if I were to tell you, Trenchard, that less than six hours ago Hale-Storford—Hale-Storford, Trenchard— was stopped from killing Dorothy Graye? What would you say if I were to tell you, too, that there is no doubt now in the minds of Scotland Yard that it was Hale-Storford—Hale-Storford, Trenchard—who was the author of all the *accidents?*"

Trenchard shot to his feet. His chair, thrust so suddenly back, fell to the carpet with a soft crash. His eyes, wide and staring, blazed into Anthony's. He put up a hand to his head.

"Hale-Storford," he said. "What are you tell·ing me, man?"

"That Hale-Storford," said Anthony quietly, "sent Miriam Rossiter to her death, and that Hale-Storford drowned young Anstruther while pretending to save him; that Hale-Storford tried to kill Miss Kerr upon three or four occasions and failed, and that Hale-Storford to-night was only just prevented from killing Dorothy Graye."

Trenchard put out a hand behind him, groping for his chair. Not finding it, the hand came back to rest heavily upon the table, supporting his weight. Still he stared at Anthony. He said in a harsh whisper:

"But you're talking madness, man! *He* couldn't have killed Eve. I know it! I know it! I was there, wasn't I? I was there just behind him when he found her. . . ."

Anthony shook his head. "I'm not saying that Hale-Storford killed his wife. No. What I'm telling you is that Hale-Storford has killed

Miriam Rossiter and George Anstruther and has tried to kill Dorothy Graye and Miss Kerr."

Trenchard gave a curious little shaking movement of his head, like a man who is trying to clear his sight. He said:

"Where—where do we get, then?"

Anthony shrugged. "Nowhere. That's the trouble. Nowhere, I mean, toward the original question: who killed Eve Hale-Storford? Hale-Storford, Trenchard, has been mad since the death of his wife. And, being mad, has tried to punish the killer of his wife, but, being mad and never quite certain that his last victim was the real criminal, he has gone on killing. He would, I'm quite certain, have eliminated all four if he hadn't been stopped."

Trenchard raised from the table one of those hands which supported him; drew its back across his eyes. He said:

"But what do you want, man? Where do we get? Good God! . . ." A sudden excitement seemed to shake his thick body. "Good God! don't you see? We're just where we started. That Graye woman!"

Anthony shook his head. "I don't believe it. No, Trenchard, I don't believe it. . . . You said, what did I want—I'll tell you what I want. I want you; I want your help." Suddenly he switched his gaze to Lucas and from Lucas to Pike. "Look here," he said, "I want us to go down to that house, taking Trenchard. Trenchard can reconstruct for us. Don't you see, Lucas—don't you see, Pike—if there's an answer to this damned riddle anywhere—and there's always an answer to any riddle—it's in that house?"

Trenchard sat heavily upon the edge of the table. "I'm game enough," he said. . . .

(8)

Susan smiled. "I feel, you know," said Susan, "really rather frighteningly unimportant. I mean, I'm not a bit used to being an anticlimax."

"You aren't," said Heath with controlled fervour.

They stood, Heath and Susan and Anthony, in the library of Susan's house. They had come

up from Little Ockleton in Anthony's car.
Somewhere, still on the road, was the police car,
in it an extra passenger, Ralph Trenchard.

Anthony set down his glass. He smiled. To
Susan he said:

"He's quite right, you know. You aren't."

."But," said Susan, "I am. Here have I, with
my accidents, and *my* kidnapping, been keeping
everybody—all the really big noises, I mean—
frightfully excited, and now, just because
they've 'cleared me up,' they go and get all bothered about something else. You know, Colonel
Gethryn, you're being very polite, but you're
not a bit interested in me now, are you?"

Anthony smiled again. "Personally, how
could I possibly help it? Problematically, not
in the least."

Susan grew suddenly grave. "I'm being rather
a little pig, you know, only this business—well,
it's so somehow awful—isn't it?—that it makes
you feel you've got to joke about it for fear of
doing something else."

Anthony nodded. "Exactly."

"And you are—" Susan was furious now;

serious and eager and quite wholly enchanting
—"and you are going down to—" she shivered a
little—"to that house?"

"The day," said Anthony, "after to-morrow.
By that time we ought to be able to take Mrs.
Graye with us as well as Trenchard. I wonder
. . ." He looked at Susan. Susan shivered again,
but she nodded bravely the golden head.

"Certainly," said Susan. "Of course I will."

"And then," said Anthony, "you needn't feel
unimportant any more, need you?"

He left them then. They came, the rest of the
household being all abed since the telephone
message of Susan's safety, to the front door and
saw him off. Just as his car started he turned.
Upon the top step they stood, very close. Susan
lifted an arm and waved. Anthony raised a hand
in salute. His big black car shot forward. They
watched the red eye of its rear light until, turning right into Pool Street, it vanished.

Susan slipped her arm through Heath's. In
silence they turned and went back into the
house.

CHAPTER NINE

LUCAS and Pike sat in the two chairs which faced each other across the hearth. Between them, facing the fire itself, were Trenchard and Susan. The three oil lamps lit the room with a hard yet yellow light. There was silence and uncomfortable silence. Pike looked at his watch.

"They've been a long time," he said.

Lucas nodded. "Yes, and we sit here like—— Well, never mind."

He stood up, a long and perhaps a little too elegant a figure. "Miss Kerr," he said. He looked toward the side table. "There's whisky there. Would you like a whisky-and-soda? Because I would, and I've no doubt Pike would, too. And you, Trenchard?"

Pike nodded. Trenchard—a silent and somehow ominous figure—shook his head.

Susan said:

"I'm afraid I would. I hate the stuff really, because they used to give me castor oil in it, but somehow—" she shivered; her small self seemed to be lost in the big chair— "somehow this room . . . Where *are* they?"

Pike jerked his head upwards. "Next floor," he said.

"I suppose," said Susan, her eyes very large. "I suppose I'm a silly little fool to feel the way—to feel——"

Pike shook his head. He was by this time another slave of Susan's.

"Not a bit you're not, Miss Kerr," he said. "Not one little bit. I ought to be hardened enough, but I don't like this place."

Lucas came back with a tumbler for Susan. "Now, Pike!" he said.

Pike grinned. "Well, sir, I'll ask you the same question. Do you like this place? Honestly, now?"

Lucas shook his head. "I don't," he said. "But what worries me is why I don't. Perhaps it's the light."

"It's not," said Susan, "the *light*."

They fell silent again; uneasily silent. . . .

Upstairs, in the small bedroom which, with its large window, seemed more like a box from out of which to look at the gray immensity of the sea; the room which had been hers for these past nine months which seemed twice that number of years, was Dorothy Graye. The window was open, the door was shut. She lay as she had been told, upon the bed. She listened. Listened, as also she had been told, with all her mind, all herself. She heard—nothing.

There came at last a tap upon her door. She swung her legs to the floor and sat up upon the edge of the bed. "Come in!" she said.

Anthony entered. There was a lamp—an old-fashioned white-globed, brass-standard oil lamp—in his right hand. Its yellow glow was soft and yet clear edged. "That's the last trial," he said. "Hear it?"

She shook her head. "I heard nothing again. Absolutely nothing."

Anthony considered this. The consideration did not seem to please him. He said after a moment:

"Right! We'll go down, then. Sure you're feeling fit for this, Mrs. Graye?"

Dorothy Graye nodded her head. "Quite," she said. Her tone was emphatic, but her looks gave the lie to what she had said. She was paler than even her usual pallor. There were under her eyes deeply impressed, black half circles.

They went downstairs.

"At last!" said Lucas. "Well?"

From a corner Anthony wheeled up, to join those in a group about the fire, a chair for his companion. He said:

"Mrs. Graye has been in her room. She has been lying down and listening. While she listened I went from every one of those other bedrooms as quietly as I could into the bedroom which was Mrs. Hale-Storford's. I stayed there for as long as need be and went back to the room from which I had come. Not in any case did Mrs. Graye hear me. Pike, you and I tried it all, every other way round, this afternoon, and you heard nothing either."

Pike nodded. "That's right, sir."

Anthony, who had not sat down, went to the

side table; poured whisky into a glass, splashed soda; brought the glass to Dorothy Graye. "Drink that," he said. "It doesn't matter if you don't like it. Drink it."

She smiled up at him wanly. She sipped; shuddered; she sipped again. A little colour began to creep back into her grayly pale cheeks.

"What's next?" said Lucas.

Anthony exhibited, most unusually, irritation. "Damn it, man, I'm thinking of that! Let's wait, shall we?"

Lucas smiled. "All right! All right! D'you know, Gethryn, if this house hadn't got the— we've been talking about it—hadn't got the feeling it has, I'd almost be inclined to like this. You're generally so certain, you know. It's quite refreshing to people like Pike and me to watch you when you aren't."

At that Anthony grinned. "Generally so certain!" he said. "I've been telling you for about twenty years that I'm never certain until just after I am." He fell grave again. He said suddenly:

"Mrs. Graye—I want to go over in my own words our conversation of this morning. I want you to listen. If I say anything wrong, pull me up, will you?"

The woman nodded. "Yes, I will."

"You have been a member of this household ever since it has been a household. You were housekeeper from the beginning to Dr. Hale-Storford and his wife. You therefore knew very well Dr. Hale-Storford and his wife. You knew, also well, Miriam Rossiter, Mrs. Hale-Storford's sister, and, not quite so well, the boy Anstruther. You must see, Mrs. Graye—we have had all this out—that if any member of the household murdered Mrs. Hale-Storford it must have been—because Banner and Trench-ard and Hale-Storford were certainly out of it—either Miss Kerr, Miss Rossiter, young Anstruther, or yourself. We know Miss Kerr didn't do it; we know that you didn't do it. . . ."

Dorothy Graye looked at him. "How?" she said.

Anthony returned the look. "I don't mean," he said, "that we can prove that either Miss

Kerr or yourself didn't do it any more than we can prove that anyone else did. But we are—" he slid a glance out of the corner of his eye at Lucas, who now had once more assumed that wooden, official mask— "prepared to back our judgment that if you or Miss Kerr had wished to get rid of Eve Hale-Storford you couldn't— and when I say couldn't I mean it—you couldn't have got rid of her in that way. Since you yourself have raised the question, I think it may be as well to answer it fully. I say that Miss Kerr, if she had wished to get rid of Eve Hale-Storford, would have done so openly and in an honest rage amounting to temporary madness. . . . Sorry, Miss Kerr, but I think I'm right. I don't say that you do have rages like that, but if you did kill anyone it would be because you did have a rage like that. . . . You, Mrs. Graye, if you had wanted to get rid of Eve Hale-Storford—don't forget my additional clause—you would do it in a far more subtle way. You could not take a knife or a razor and cut someone's throat."

Anthony was speaking very slowly. The last

four words of the last sentence came out separately and heavy; they dropped into the dead silence of the room like stones into a dark, deep pool. He said, after a pause, a pause whose lack of sound was broken only by the sharp hissing intake of breath from Susan:

"Also, Mrs. Graye—" his green eyes were staring down into the woman's— "also, Mrs. Graye, I have no reason for saying this except my judgment, but I think that you are afraid of blood. . . ."

The woman in the chair straightened suddenly her long body. She sat rigid, bracing her back against the chair's back. Her left hand clutched the chair's arm until the knuckles showed dead white against her skin. Her right hand, palm outward, suddenly covered her eyes. "Don't!" she said. "Don't!"

"Thought so," said Anthony. His words were now normal both in tone and speed. "We are left then with Miriam Rossitor and George Anstruther as possibles. Going over our conversation of this morning, I think that you, as the person out of all of us who knew these

other persons best, cannot adduce any reason
for either of these two persons wishing to get
rid of Eve Hale-Storford, or for either of these
two persons—even if have a reason they did—
to do so in such a manner. Is that right?"

Still with that hand pressed against her eyes
Dorothy Graye nodded.

"We are therefore," Anthony went on,
"exactly where we started months ago. We have
four possibles; four only. We know that it can't
have been either Hale-Storford himself or
Trenchard or Banner, and we can assume that it
was not under any circumstances an outsider.
The probabilities are so dead against any other
assumption. There is only one thing left. . . ."

Trenchard started in his chair and spoke. It
was the first movement and the first sound,
almost, which he had made since their entry
into that room more than an hour before. Under
his black poll his heavy face showed shockingly
white. He said:

"There's *nothing* left, you mean. Nothing!"

His eyes, which had been on Anthony at the
beginning of his speech, flickered sideways,

rested their glance for one almost unappreci-
able second upon the woman Graye.

Anthony shook his head. "No, one thing left,
Trenchard, and when every other possible
thing's exhausted, the one thing left must be the
right answer. You know that. . . . Child's
Guide to Logic. . . There were five persons
that night upstairs, and if none of the other four
killed Eve Hale-Storford, Eve Hale-Storford
must have killed herself."

Another silence, broken this time by Lucas.
And Lucas said, losing for the moment his
officialdom and becoming an ordinary, intelligent, but much puzzled man:

"I've been saying that to myself, Gethryn—
and I expect everybody else has—at the end of
every sequence of thought about this business,
right from the beginning. But—" he levered
himself from his chair and crossed the room
to face Anthony before the fireplace—"but,
Gethryn, when you've said that, it's no more
sense than any of the rest of this business. No
human being can cut his own throat in the way
that throat was cut and then hide the instrument

with which the wound was made. And hide it, mind you, so that not even the most extensive search can find it. Have you ever read the description of that wound? The description of how the body was lying when it was found?"

Trenchard, stirring uneasily in his chair, had taken a handkerchief from his pocket and was passing it across his forehead. From Dorothy Graye there came a moan: "Don't Please don't!"

"Sorry," said Lucas, "sorry! But I suppose you people knew what you were likely to have to go through when you consented to come down here." He was not sympathetic.

Anthony looked at him. "My dear Lucas! It appears obviously impossible for Eve Hale-Storford, if kill herself she did, to have hidden her weapon. But it does not, at least not yet to me, appear impossible that *anyone else should have done so. . . ."*

The silence which followed these last words of Anthony's was broken by Pike. Pike, who jumped to his feet and said:

"My Gosh, sir!" and then lost immediately

all elation. But he went on: "I've been all over this house myself, sir, and before that— on the very night of the death, in fact—the local police had been all over it themselves. That's so, isn't it, sir?" He looked at Trenchard.

Trenchard nodded. The laugh he gave was like the laugh he had given in his own house three nights before; a sound most distressing to hear. "All over it! Short of setting fire to the place and raking about in the ashes, they did everything."

Once more his eyes which had had, it seemed, meant to fix themselves upon Pike's, slid sideways to the form, half sitting, half lying in the chair next his own, of Dorothy Graye. He added, before anyone else could speak:

"But razors have been cleaned, you know. And there is running water."

Anthony spoke. His words came hard upon the heels of Trenchard's, but they seemed to have no relation to Trenchard's. They were:

"I want you to tell me, Mrs. Graye—and this is a question I haven't asked you before— whether you know of any reason why Eve Hale-

Storford should have wanted to kill herself. I'm sorry if this is painful, but it can't be helped."

The woman let the hand which had been covering her eyes drop into her lap. It dropped like a dead weight. "None," she said. "None."

"There's one person," said Lucas, "who might answer that question, but he can't. He can't answer any question."

Anthony nodded. "Yes. Hale-Storford's madness holds us up. . . . Or not, Lucas. Or not." He turned again to Dorothy Graye. He said:

"Mrs. Graye, did you notice anything—I know you've been asked these questions before, and I know your answer to them, but I'm asking them again—did you notice anything about Eve Hale-Storford on the day preceding the night of her death which might show that she was in an abnormal condition of mind?"

Once more the head was shaken. "No, nothing."

Anthony sat himself down upon the edge of the padded fender. Now his eyes were more nearly on a level with the woman's. They looked, their greenness most pronounced, almost fiercely into hers. "Nothing?" he said. *"Nothing at all?"*

She met the gaze, raising her head proudly. "Nothing," she said deliberately. "Nothing at——" and then checked. Like a flash Anthony pounced.

"There *was* something, then? All right, Mrs. Graye, I'm not trying to 'catch you out,' I'm trying to help you. You've just—it's no good trying to say you haven't—remembered some little thing which until now you'd either forgotten altogether or thought unworthy of mention. That right?"

Once more the right hand of Dorothy Graye pressed its back against her eyes. From under the hand she spoke. She said:

"I don't know. . . ."

"Tell me," said Anthony slowly, "what you don't know."

The woman's left hand came up to join her right. Both the hands pressed themselves against her forehead. She said:

"It's only that that morning at breakfast I thought Eve had been crying."

Lucas swung round on her. "You've never said that before, Mrs. Graye." His tone was sharp, almost menacing. He looked at Anthony; met so ferocious a glare from Anthony's eyes that he fell silent. Anthony said quickly:

"Never mind that, Mrs. Graye. Tell me."

"I never thought of it before. I never thought of it before. It was so—I think it was a silly idea of mine. Because—because—well, no sooner had I noticed it—it's all coming back to me now—no sooner had I noticed it than Eve seemed to become her usual very happy self again. I thought perhaps I'd made a silly mistake. In fact, I didn't think I'd made a silly mistake, I knew I had, or thought I knew."

Anthony, who had risen, sat himself down upon the fender. Again he looked steadily into the woman's eyes. Her hands once more were in her lap. Once more she seemed to steel herself to meet his glance.

"Mrs. Graye," said Anthony, "was there, to your knowledge, any woman member of this household besides his wife who was in love with Hale-Storford?"

"Yes," said Dorothy Graye. At this answer the eyes of the others in that room came round to her. She went on staring at Anthony. She was rigid.

"Miriam Rossiter?" said Anthony.

The woman shook her head. "No. Myself."

"And was," said Anthony, his tone as emotionless as his face, "any person in the house other than yourself aware of this?"

"No," said the woman.

Now Anthony's level voice cut the silence like a sharp but gently wielded knife. "So that, Mrs. Graye, the reason for the possible unhappiness of Mrs. Hale-Storford could not have been yourself?"

"No," said the woman. No part of her moved save her hands. These clenched and unclenched their long fingers as they lay in her lap.

"And did you, Mrs. Graye, know anything of the death of Eve Hale-Storford before that death was discovered by Eve Hale-Storford's husband?"

"No," said the woman. Her pallor was now so ghastly that Susan leaned forward, anguished, her eyes fixed upon that ashen face.

"You did not, then," the calm, cold voice went on, "find by some accident that Eve Hale-Storford had killed herself? You did not, having thus found, remove the weapon and hide it with the idea of saving some pain at least to the dead woman's husband who was also the man you loved?"

"No," said the woman.

Anthony's eyes remained on hers during the silence which followed. Then, suddenly, with a change somehow in the whole of his aspect he got to his feet.

"Thank you," he said. "I have been no doubt insulting. I will go on being insulting to this extent, that I will say that I believe every word you've said."

He turned his back on her. He said to Lucas:

"There's one thing now we can do. And if that fails, as it probably will fail, I for one give this thing up."

(2)

"You will *please,*" said Anthony twenty minutes later, "stay here. Are you all right, Mrs.

Graye? Miss Kerr, look after her, won't you?"

Susan nodded. "But will you," said Susan, her eyes enormous in a pale face, "will you, please, shut the door?"

Anthony smiled at her. "Of course we will. And we'll all be just upstairs, you know."

He opened the door. He went out into the pitch black and somehow abnormally thick-seeming darkness of the hall. He called:

"Ready, Lucas?" and then waited. No answer came.

He went to the foot of the stairs and called again louder:

"Ready, Lucas?" Again no answer. Pike appeared at his shoulder. "Good Lord, sir," said Pike, "What——"

"Ready Lucas?" Anthony's voice was now a shout.

An answer came. At Anthony's shoulder Pike sighed relief.

"Ready," came Lucas's voice, very faint.

"Well, hold it till we get there." Anthony turned to Pike. "Come back now."

They went back, not into the drawing room

where were the two women, but into the room which had been, until he had begun to use the Watch Tower, Hale-Storford's study. In this room, pacing up and down before the cold blank hearth, was Trenchard. Anthony shut the door behind himself and Pike. The three men looked at each other in silence. The wide window of this room stood open, and faintly through the darkness there came to their ears the soft hiss-hishing of the sea against the rocks below.

"Ready, Trenchard?" said Anthony at last.

Trenchard nodded. He said, moistening his lips with his tongue:

"Frightful job!"

"Come on," said Anthony, "and don't forget —I'm Hale-Storford, you're yourself, Pike's Banner. We go out, me first, you second, Pike third. I take the lamp. . . . Oh, by the way, Pike, go and light that lamp on the hall table."

Pike went.

"I take the lamp," said Anthony again, "and I go upstairs. I am going to show you and Banner to your rooms."

Trenchard nodded.

"We walk as quietly as we can down the corridor, still in the same order. As Hale-Storford I stop outside my own door. I say something to you; you see what you saw. I dash into the room. . . ."

Again Trenchard nodded. He said:

"What then?"

"Lucas," said Anthony, "is lying on the bed as nearly as possible in the position of Eve Hale-Storford. . . . Sorry, Trenchard, but you said you'd do this."

"Go on!" said Trenchard between his teeth. "I'm all right!"

"Lucas has got in his hand a bit of firewood about the size of an ordinary razor. What we're going to try is this. I'm going to see if I can take that out of his hand, which is clenched tight, and put it into my pocket, hidden, within the time which Hale-Storford had at his disposal. That's to say, before he came back to the door again. You've got to use your judgment, Trenchard. So soon as you want me as Hale-Storford back at the door to make things right—or half a second before that—you must say, 'Now!' When you've said, 'Now,' I shall stop trying, whether I've succeeded or not, and come back to the door. Got that?"

Trenchard nodded. Pike came back into the room.

"We will go," said Anthony. "You know, don't you, Pike? You're Banner and you keep behind."

Pike nodded.

Anthony, the lamp held shoulder high, mounted the stairs, behind him Trenchard, behind Trenchard, Pike. The old house, except for sudden creakings and raps and the sound of their footfalls, was deadly quiet. The lamp's yellow flood—now circular, now elliptic, now distorted by contact with this wall and that corner—mounted steadily. . . . The three stood at the top of the stairs. Anthony turned left. He said, speaking his lines:

"First door's my sister-in-law's. . . . This one's Susan Kerr's. . . . This next one's Eve's and mine."

Outside the third door on the right he halted. He said:

"There are your two, next each other."

Into Pike's ribs Trenchard's elbow was driven. Pike did his part; said:

"Gosh man! What's up?"

Anthony swung round. The pool of light widened in a flickering circle. Trenchard was staring at the floor. Not at that part of the floor immediately beneath his feet or his comrades', but at the boards which were, just inside the circle of the lamp's light, outside the bedroom door of Eve Hale-Storford. In the yellow glow his face showed as a pallid blotch. As he stared his right arm rose—slowly, seemingly without volition—to point a rigid finger.

"What's up?" His voice was a harsh, strident whisper.

Pike drew in his breath. "Water," he said. "It's water. Somebody's spilt some water."

Anthony left them. They stood there in the darkness. Anthony was at the door, and with him was the light. The doorway was bathed in the soft flood. Anthony set his fingers to the door handle; flung open the door. The others heard his voice: "Eve!" he said. "Eve!"

Then there was silence. . . .

Just as upon that night nine months ago Trenchard had grasped the arm of old Banner with fingers of iron, so now he gripped Pike's. He stared into the room. Pike stared too. They could see a little; the door was open. They could see, reflected from the white ceiling, the yellow flood of the lamp.

Softly to himself, with his breath coming hard and fast, Trenchard began to count. "One" . . . he said—"Two . . . three . . . four . . . five . . . *Now,* Gethryn!"

. . . And then Anthony was at the door again. They went to him. He shrugged.

"Did you get it?" said Trenchard hoarsely.

Anthony shook his head. "No," he said. "Could have in another couple of seconds. I was allowing time, of course, for being pulled up by the shock of the first sight."

Now out of the darkness came Lucas, straightening a rumpled coat. In his hand was a piece of wood about the size of a single-blade razor of the old-fashioned kind. Anthony handed the lamp to Pike.

"We'll go down now," he said.

They went down again and presently stood once more before the blank dismal hearth in the study.

"And that," said Anthony, "is that."

"I thought," said Lucas despondently, "that it would be. We'll never get anywhere on this, Gethryn. Never! Damn it, it's a sort of *Marie Céleste* business!"

"Here's a thing, sir," said Pike. He looked with some diffidence at Anthony. He thought that Colonel Gethryn had probably already seen this point, but bravely he put it.

"If Mrs. Hale-Storford had dropped the thing she killed herself with, then Hale-Storford would have had time to hide it."

"Yes, Pike," Anthony nodded. "But if Mrs. Hale-Storford killed herself with a razor or a knife, something that she could get a grip on, that grip would not loosen. And if it didn't loosen, it would tighten. You know that."

Pike nodded, rather despondently. "Yes, there's that, sir. And, by Gosh! there's something I'd forgotten. There's the fact that if he had shoved this razor or whatever it was into his pocket, there'd have been blood, wouldn't there? And I think Mr. Trenchard will bear me out that the local police included even clothes in their search."

Trenchard had walked over to the window. He stood now with his broad back toward them, hands in his pockets, staring out into the darkness. Without turning round he said:

"Yes, that's quite right. All our clothes."

"And I think," said Anthony, "that the number of old-fashioned razors in this house is just two. That right, Pike?"

Pike nodded. "Yes, sir. One of the boy Anstruther's—queer thing, a lot of boys seem to like the old type; makes 'em feel more manly, I suppose—and one of Hale-Storford's himself. Both tidy, both clean, both in the bathroom.

"And they," said Anthony, "were the only suitable weapons in the house?"

Pike nodded. "No knives of the right type, sir. No nothing. Dr. Hale-Storford had another razor, but it was one of those little Sambak safeties, and that was all tidy, all neat, and in the bathroom. Not that it could have been used, anyhow."

Lucas stretched his arms. "This thing will drive us all mad!" he said.

Trenchard spoke from the window, still without turning. "Perhaps we all are!" he said. His voice was higher than usual, and there was a harsh, strident sound about it.

Anthony began to pace the room, up and down the square of carpet in its centre. He said, pacing:

"Let's just see that we *have* got nowhere. We've shown that it's almost impossible, if Eve Hale-Storford killed herself, for her husband to have concealed her weapon. So, like the original problem of *murder,* we're back again with those four upstairs people—Dorothy Graye, Anstruther, Susan Kerr, and Miriam Rossiter."

"And," Lucas interrupted, "we can't tell, any more than we could when we were thinking of murder, about Anstruther or the Rossiter woman. Your experiments with Pike and Mrs.

Graye show that anyone could have gone from any one of the rooms to Eve Hale-Storford's room and back again without being heard. Anstruther and Rossiter are dead. Susan Kerr and Dorothy Graye are alive. We say that we believe Susan Kerr and Dorothy Graye, and so we are left with the possibility—the utterly unprovable possibility—that either Anstruther or Rossiter discovered Eve Hale-Storford's suicide and hid the proof of it. . . . It's no good, Gethryn, you can try and make us think it's suicide, or we can think it's murder. Whichever way we look at it, we're no forrader."

Anthony was still pacing the carpet. His head was downbent, his shoulders hunched; a frown carved deep lines into his forehead. He said, stopping suddenly in his walk:

"I say, Trenchard!"

Trenchard turned. He leaned back now against the wall beside the window. He looked, and was, a man utterly weary. He said in a dead voice:

"Yes? What do you want?"

"Just one thing," said Anthony. "Did we do

that reconstruction without any mistakes at all?
Think before you answer. Without any mistakes at all?"

Trenchard thought, closing heavy-lidded
eyes. His white face against the dark wall
looked like a death mask. He said at last, opening his eyes:

"Nothing. Nothing that I can remember."

Anthony drew closer to him. "Sure?" he
said.

Trenchard nodded. "Sure!"

"And there was," said Anthony, "if not anything wrong, nothing in any way different about
the proceeding? Think please! Think like all
hell!"

Once more Trenchard closed his eyes and
thought.

Lucas came to Anthony's side. "What're you
after now?" he said in a whisper.

Anthony, not taking his eyes off Trenchard,
shrugged. "God knows!" he said. "But I'm on
the only line left to us. Not much of a
one. . . ."

Trenchard's eyes opened. He shook his head.

"Nothing," he said. . . . "Wait though! . . . Oh, but that's trivial!"

"What's trivial?" said Anthony quietly. "Better say."

Trenchard shrugged weary shoulders. "Just that it was all so much *quieter*. But that's because of the carpets being down now. *That* night there was no stair carpet and no carpet in Hale-Storford's room. Nothing else different— not that my mind registers, anyhow. Sorry!"

"Thanks," said Anthony. He threw himself angrily into a chair. He looked up at Lucas and then at Pike. He said:

"Well, we're beat, aren't we? . . . D'you know what's frightening me?" He spoke in a low voice. He seemed not to want his words to carry to Trenchard.

Lucas said nothing. Pike looked enquiry.

"What's frightening me," said Anthony, still low, "is the thought of how this damned thing, just as a problem, is going to nag at my mind and nag at it and never give me any peace. Blast it!"

"We've got to forget it, I suppose," said

Lucas. "If we do that something will perhaps go and turn up some day." His tone was far from hopeful.

Pike shook his head gloomily, looking at his boots. "Not in this case it won't, sir. You mark my words——"

He broke off suddenly, staring at Anthony. Anthony was leaning forward in his chair. His lips were a little parted, his green eyes blazing fire.

"My God!" he said under his breath.

"What's that, sir? What's that?" Lucas took a step forward. "What's up, Gethryn?" He got no answer, save the crash of the suddenly opened door as it swung back against the wall. . . . Anthony was gone.

On quick feet Pike was at the door, saw Anthony's tall figure at the table by the lamp, saw him raise the lamp and go upstairs running four at a time. He turned an eager face to Lucas: "He's onto something, sir. Come on!"

They went up the stairs, but they could not run. The lamp was gone, and they had to feel their way. It seemed suddenly cold upon the stairs. Quite cold and very dark. The darkness seemed to be pushing at them, pushing them back. Each man could hear the other's laboured breathing as he reached the top. They looked down the corridor. From the door of the room which had been the dead woman's a light gleamed. They walked toward it. As they reached the threshold Anthony came out. He ran into them.

"Pike!" he said, and his voice sent Pike running, in spite of the darkness. "Nip downstairs and find something like a cold chisel. Anything that will do for a lever, strong and with a thin edge. Hurry, man!"

He turned back into the room. Lucas followed him. Lucas saw that the carpet, the big, thick pile carpet, had been rolled back. The bed, too —the bed upon which Lucas just now in rather dreadful imitation had lain—was pulled aside. The old dark floor boards gave back faint reflection of lamplight. By the bed, on these bare boards, Anthony dropped upon his knees.

"What the devil——" Lucas began.

"Shut up!" said Anthony from the floor.

"Here, get that light and put it down here, will you?"

Lucas obeyed. Anthony, with a sudden lithe twist, was no longer kneeling but flat upon his face. "Light a bit nearer," he grunted. "Bit to the right . . . bit to the left . . . there, hold it!"

"What the devil——" said Lucas. He was kneeling now. He heard Anthony murmuring to himself beneath his breath but could catch no words. There came the sound of feet in the corridor outside, and then with a little stumble Pike was in the room again. In his hand he held a cold chisel and a mallet. "These do, sir?" he said.

Anthony rolled over to one side and climbed to his knees. "That'll do. Here, have this board up. This one here."

Pike stooped to look, saw that the floor board indicated was the one which ran alongside the bed's normal position, and saw, too, a board whose aged edge, cracked and chipped, was gaping along nearly a foot of its length nearly an inch away from its fellow. Moved by an excitement but not quite knowing himself its cause, he set to work. . . .

With a little crashing scream the board came up.

"Lamp!" said Anthony. "Lamp!" Once more he lay upon his face. They pushed the lamp toward him along the floor. Into the yawning foot-wide slit he peered, his face level with the floor. "Well, well!" he said. He laughed, a hard sound. He thrust down into the pit a long arm; he groped. Presently, almost in one movement, he levered himself to his feet.

Lucas lifted the lamp. He and Pike gazed open mouthed, understanding flooding slowly into their minds. Upon Anthony's outstretched hand—a hand covered with gray-black dust and strands of ancient cobweb—lay something which dully and rustily reflected a few specks of golden light from the lamp. A small something. A something an inch in length by an inch and a half in breadth.

"See it?" said Anthony in a voice unlike his own. "See it? Know what it is, don't you? . . . That's a Sambak razor blade. Look!"

They pored over his hand.

"Great Jing!" said Pike. "Mean to say, sir——"

"Yes, Gethryn, what exactly do you mean?" Lucas's tone was impatient. He knew, or thought he knew, but wanted confirmation.

"Take this," said Anthony. He thrust the fouled hand forward and tipped the blade into Lucas's palm. "Got it, haven't you? The explanation, I mean? It was just that one thing Trenchard said just now that gave it to me. . . . Well, not gave it to me, but put me for the first time onto the extraordinary possibility. He said there was a carpet here now—this carpet— which wasn't there when the woman died. A few minutes before he said that Pike said something about a Sambak razor. Now, I know Sambaks, I've used one. They're not English, but they're good. They've only got, Lucas, *one edge*. That's to say, you can hold them and do things with them without cutting yourself with them the way you would with an ordinary double-edged blade. . . .

"Eve Hale-Storford did kill herself! . . .

Look where that crack was, man. That crack an inch wide. She killed herself; she slumped forward as she had made the wound in her throat. . . ." He sat himself down upon the bed and went through a mummery ghastly in its accuracy of the actions he was describing.

"See, like that across her throat . . . like this tumbling forward; like this, right hand forward. . . . Then, because this blade isn't a thing you could grip but have to hold between finger and thumb, it falls out of her hand and down into that crack in the floor."

From Pike's pursed lips there came a long and almost soundless whistle. "That's it, sir!" he said. "That's it!"

Lucas, bending near the lamp, was looking at the blade. "They can tell us," he was saying, "whether this is blood or not."

"They will," said Anthony. "That's all right, Lucas."

Lucas looked up. "By God!" he said. "I believe you're right. But why, man, why? What on earth does a girl like that want to go and cut her throat for?"

Anthony shrugged. "That's a thing I'll never know. But I'll make a guess for you, if you like."

Lucas looked at him. "Which is?"

Anthony rose from the bed's edge. "Which is this, Lucas. You've heard the Graye woman—the woman you've never until now quite ceased to suspect—you have heard her tell about that instance when she thought the happy young wife had been crying? Haven't you?"

Lucas nodded.

"And you heard her say that so far as she knew there was no cause for jealousy on that young wife's part?"

Again Lucas nodded, slowly this time, as a man will nod who thinks he has seen the point but may not be quite sure.

"And you saw," said Anthony, "three days ago, Hale-Storford sitting on the quay side, a gibbering, witless thing, didn't you?"

Lucas nodded, decisively this time.

"It seems," said Anthony slowly, "to me that when a rather neurotic girl whose life is made up of her love for a man suddenly finds that

that man, although he has hidden it from the world and himself and her for all this time, is insane and will do nothing in life except to grow more insane——"

He broke off suddenly. "Not much good, our theorizing, is it? But it is a theory, and a possible one."

"And, sir," said Pike, "I should think the right one."

Lucas shrugged. He always strove not to show Pike's faith. He said:

"Well, anyhow, we'll never get there."

He looked round the room. "Let's go down, shall we?" he said.

Anthony nodded. "Yes. Not so pleasant up here, is it?"

In single file, Pike leading, holding the lamp above his head, they left the room.

(3)

Susan, her small face white, her eyes big lakes of horror, stared at Anthony. They stood, alone, just within the drawing-room door. From the hall came the sound of voices as Lucas and

Pike, Trenchard helping, carried the other woman out to the waiting car.

Anthony nodded. He said:

"Yes. *She's* the tragedy, you know."

Susan shuddered. "Oh, but it's all so awful and so—so——"

"Unnecessary," said Anthony.

She nodded the golden head. "Yes. Think of that poor boy and poor Miriam, dead for—for —it would be horrible anyhow, but dead for— for—a mistake."

"And think," said Anthony gravely, "of Hale-Storford himself. It's difficult, I know, but he's to be pitied."

Susan hid her face in her hands. She seemed to be shaking her head.

"I know," said Anthony. "It is difficult."

Susan raised her face again. "If only one could—could *do* something," she said.

Anthony smiled at her. "One can," he said. "Especially you."

"You mean?" Susan's tone was eager. She stared up at him.

Anthony nodded. "Exactly. Dorothy Graye.

I said just now she's the pitiful one, because, you know, she's loved Hale-Storford all this time. Now, you can do something about her, can't you? And there's nothing like doing something, you know, to get nastinesses out of one's mind. And nastinesses, if you don't mind my saying so, oughtn't to worry anything so charming as that head! Now, come along!"

He led the way out into the darkness of the hall and so through the great studded oaken door into the night. On the threshold he turned, caught the loop of iron in the door's centre and slammed it close. Susan shuddered; pressed herself against his side. He put a hand on her arm and guided her up to the steep gravel path to the gate which led onto the road. . . .

The Watch House, empty and alone, stared out, as it had stared out for three hundred years, across the night and the sea.

FINIS